William Maltese's

FLICKER

#1 BOOK OF ANSWERS

I0671754

Savant Books and Publications
Honolulu, HI
2010

Published in the USA by Savant Books and
Publications
2630 Kapiolani Blvd #1601
Honolulu, HI 96826
http://www.savantbooksandpublications.com

Printed in the USA

Edited by Daniel S. Janik
Images and Front Cover design by John U. Abrahamson
(www.JohnUA.com)
Back Cover design by Daniel S. Janik

ISBN-13: 978-0-9845552-4-6
ISBN-10: 0-9845552-4-2

DEDICATION

To Jfay whose candles (flickering flames, "read" or otherwise) are always an inspiration.

Table of Contents

William Maltese's

FLICKER

#1 BOOK OF ANSWERS

AUTHOR'S NOTE

There is a long-held history in our family from a time, many years before I was born, when certain of us possessed the power of candle-reading divination, all of which faded at one and the same time Major Magic made its inexplicable exit from the world. Ever since, those of us, like me, have been relegated by friends and society to divining the future from the way steaming entrails of sacrificed animals are spilled upon slabs of cold stone, or the future from the patterns of migrating birds, and more recently, parlor tricks like mind-reading, picking correct cards from a deck, trying to decipher meaning from within crystal balls, the deal of the Tarot, a throw of dice, the lines on the palm of a hand; and, finally, twice a year, to the lighting of a ritual candle *in memoriam* of those long-gone, long-lost, mostly forgotten candle-readers.

Except . . . at the last biyearly lighting of a ritual candle, I truly experienced a vision, and since then, with each candle-lighting subsequent visions. All of which leads me to believe that I have been chosen, by whomever or whatever powers may be, to chronicle not only the reasons behind the initial fading of Major Magic but also its recent return.

So, join me, if you will, as I light yet another candle, one made specifically for this purpose by the candle-artisan, Jfay, and begin recording for posterity, and relating to you, personally, what is even now occurring, at this very moment, in an area around a small town called Flicker in central Washington State, where there is, even as I write, fierce competition in progress between young and old, male and female, candle-readers, vampires, werewolves, shape-shifters, demons, dragons, shadow-people, chimera, tree-spirits, and all manner of other long forgotten beasts and races, some once known, some never known, but all vying for the ultimate power in Major Magic—sitting on the Master Magician's throne.

I light my candle within this dim-lit room. I relax and let myself merge with the flame, dance within its flickering glow. I gaze into its fiery center to read what is my family's heritage and my own present and future to see.

And, this is what I see...

#1 DREAM A LITTLE DREAM

Melissa Remoth had dreamed the dream before.

The first time was the night she turned thirteen, and she has continued to dream it, on and off, for three years.

The landscape through which she walks is bleak, but familiar. It is, in fact, the area surrounding the town of Flicker, a maze of crazily-shaped barren rocks, disjoined boulders, and deep gullies, all resulting from gigantic prehistoric floods that ripped through the area thousands of years before.

Melissa's parents, both geologists, have been researching the area for years. They specifically moved to Flicker well before Melissa was born, in order to devote their time to studying the strange and often unique formations and put a scientific explanation to them. Even before Melissa could talk or walk, she had been taken by her mother and father on constant field trips into the ancient flood lands.

In her recurring dream—and she knows it's a dream—she recognizes exactly where she is. She's visited Dry Wash Gulch countless times before, awake and in sleep. The well-worn riverbed of ancient basaltic stone, long-ago carved by rushing flood waters, leads the way past a gigantic slab of volcanic glass at which she now stops, as she always does, to examine her moonlight reflection in the black obsidian.

She wears a red robe and hood. She pulls back the latter and shakes out her long, blond hair. Somehow, despite the darkness of the night, her clear blue eyes reflect back in the endless black of the stone.

Here, the dream changes from that which is intimately familiar to something entirely new: She reaches out a hand and touches her reflection in the icy cold surface and a sighing of stone-against-stone issues to her right.

She turns to see a cleft with a pathway that hasn't been there before.

Unable to stop herself, she moves along the revealed trail deeper into darkness. Though she's afraid she'll trip on the rough and unfamiliar stones underfoot, she successfully maneuvers all obstacles until...

The cavern in which she is standing has a niche filled with a large stack of candles. Somehow, she suspects, it all has something to do with her mother, who makes unusual candles as a hobby.

Without thinking, she reaches out and pulls one conveniently-placed candle from the pile, and stands it upright on an adjacent block of stone. In the pocket of her robe, she finds a lighter and sets fire to the wick...

Shadows flicker on the wall. The candle flame shimmers in the distorted light and dark to—quite miraculously—assume human form: a girl, no older than Melissa, with dark eyes and hair. She wears a long, blue robe. Her mouth moves, but there's no sound.

"What?" Melissa asks and leans closer.

The apparition's lips move again, this time managing a whispered, "How long?"

Melissa hasn't a clue as to the proper response.

The girl morphs back into a candle flame.

The fire held by the wick sputters, then goes out.

Melissa awakes with a start in her own bedroom.

#2 THE GIRL, THE CAVE, AND THE CANDLES

Melissa has always known exactly what she's supposed to do. More than once, she has been given explicit instructions. Nonetheless, she is reluctant to crawl from within her cocooning warm blankets and enter the chill beyond. Though the furnace is on—she can hear the blower at work in the basement trying to prevent the water pipes from freezing—the thermostat is always turned down at bed time.

Still…

Finally…

She throws back the blankets and sheet, and reaches for her robe. Her feet shuffle to find and finally enter the confining warmth of her slippers waiting just beneath the edge of the bed.

There is enough filtered light through the blinds

from a dawn, somewhere lost on the horizon, that she doesn't need to switch on any lights.

She leaves her room for the dimmer hallway, passing her older sister's room. Through the door, she can hear Trish breathing regularly.

The door to her parents' room is open; she can just barely make out her parents' king-size bed.

She taps lightly on the doorjamb. "Mom? Dad?"

Her mother, the lighter sleeper, responds. "Melissa, baby?"

"It's about the dream, Mom. It came back but was different this time."

There is immediate movement within the room. Mary Remoth's bedside light clicks on revealing the twist of her body reaching for the light. The woman scoots into a sitting position; blankets pool in her lap revealing the top of a pink flannel nightgown. A slender, comely woman, at five-foot-one and one-hundred-ten pounds, she looks very small in the large bed.

Beside her, Roger Remoth stirs. Athletically large and imposing, he reflexively moves a wrist to shield his closed eyes from the artificial illumination without waking up.

Mary pats a position on the bed's edge, beside her, inviting her younger daughter deeper into the bedroom.

Melissa *en route*, Mary shifts her husband's hand away from his eyes.

"Wake up, Roger. There's been a dream shift."

Melissa is surprised at how quickly her father responds. Like water from a breaching whale, his blankets slide down his torso as far as his pajama waistband, to display the exquisite muscles of his lightly-haired chest. The hands-on owner of Remoth Construction, Roger's usually well-honed body appears even more so after a summer spent building the new Flicker High School, as well as in erecting several new houses at the Rocky Shores and Pinacle Point development projects. The ripple of his muscles always leaves Melissa feeling exceptionally safe.

Roger wipes the sleep from his eyes—which are the same startling blue as those of his younger daughter —as his daughter sits on the edge of the bed in the place made by her mother.

"Tell us what you dreamed, honey," Mary prods.

Melissa does as asked.

"You're sure the candle you lit and the girl's robe were both blue?" Mary asks.

"Yes." After a moment, Melissa adds, "Should I have known the answer to what she asked?"

"Though she doesn't yet know it, honey, she's the only one who has the answer she wants."

"I don't understand," Melissa admits.

"There's a good deal we still need to tell you and likely should have," Mary apologizes. "We were hoping this would pass you by, as it did my generation; as it did many generations before."

"In the meantime, we have to get dressed and drive to Dry Wash Gulch," Roger says.

"You think the cave, the candles, and the girl in blue are really there?" Melissa asks with definite surprise.

"Maybe not where you dreamed them, honey," Mary says, "but they're there, somewhere. We must do our best to find them before the others do."

"Others?"

"The bad guys," Mary better defines.

"It's going to be okay, honey," Roger assures. He reaches for his daughter's nearest hand and enfolds it within both of his larger ones.

"The powers of good will surely be on our side," he says and kisses Melissa's cool fingertips.

#3 WINDOW TO WHERE?

A flash, a glow, a maturely elongated flame—vague images begin to swirl within, wildly, one after another.

Sixteen-year old Timothy Gril slides his welt-striated back and buttocks down the rough wall in one corner of the room. Reaching a squat, he places his elbows on his knees and hides his face in his hands, leaving the smallest of spaces between his fingers to see with his pale green eyes, careful not to touch his split lip, or his black eye. A tousle of red hair cascades over his forehead, momentarily concealing the large and growing bruise.

Gyle Gril, Timothy's father, paces the other side of the room in front of the boy. A tic periodically pulls the man's left cheek momentarily into an agitated and evil grin. His large hands, their fingernails never quite cleaned after each day's work in the water reclamation project that's turning Flicker into a constantly enlarging, scab-lands oasis, open and close tensely. The pulse spot at the base of his thick neck reveals his racing heartbeat.

"Don't you dare move from there!" Gyle threatens, pointing a menacing finger at his son as he abruptly stops pacing.

Simultaneously, a popping sound issues from the glass panes in the sliding door to the side of father and son. The sudden change in air pressure suggests an imminent hurricane. For a moment, father and son hear the outside wind howl.

Gyle races to the sliding glass door and throws it open to the darkness outside just in time for Gregory Ranlin to enter gracefully through the breach. His six-foot frame, bent to achieve entrance, easily unfolds. He runs a hand through his long, black hair to make it automatically fall into order.

"So," Gregory says, black eyes set within his extraordinarily handsome face, having surveyed the scene within the room.

"Timothy knew, all right," Gyle announces. He repeats, as if unheard the first time. "Just as you said he would. I found *that* . . ." He motions toward a small cloth-wrapped bundle on one cushion of the couch, ". . . in the back of his closet." Gyle goes over and unfolds the cloth package roughly with distaste. Inside there's a distorted lump of gray and black wax which may, or may not, have once been a candle.

"Why don't you leave your son and me alone for a few minutes, Gyle?" Gregory says.

"You want me to leave the room?" Obviously, Gyle finds the request surprising and, glancing at his son's only partially-hidden marks from the beating necessary to force the information from the boy, not at all to his liking.

"Yes, please," Gregory says. His voice is low, his

tone polite, but there's something in the tone of his voice that insinuates he won't accept refusal.

Gyle storms out of the living room, stomping down the hall to enter his bedroom, then slams the door loudly.

"Well, then," Gregory says. He positions a chair to better face Timothy's corner and sits. Pursing his full lips, he tents his two index fingers and places the resulting apex within the deep cleft of his chin. "I think it's time I apologize to you, my boy. Hopefully, it's not too late to make a difference. I'm afraid my fondness for your father and my inability to believe this would happen in our lifetimes has caused me to be terribly neglectful in seeing that you are properly cared for. I'm going to try and rectify that, beginning here and now. First, however, I need you to tell me what you saw in the candle flame; then I can tell you how to make your life easier, at least, from here on out."

He waits.

Timothy silently eyes the handsome and dark-complexioned visitor through the tiny slits between the fingers still covering his beaten face.

"You envisioned a girl, possibly one of your classmates, walking the scrublands," Gregory offers when Timothy remains silent. "You're not too sure which classmate, because candle-reading skills, even

11

among the few of our kind who have them, are never entirely clear. Yes?"

Still, Timothy does nothing but stay crouched, watching.

"This girl enters a cave and finds some candles, one of which she lights. Shortly thereafter she is joined by a second girl who, like the first, seems familiar but is not entirely recognizable to you. I assume this was all visualized in black-and-white, of course, since no candle-reader on our side these days has access to a full color palette."

Gregory leans back more fully into his chair and folds his arms across his chest. The creases of his black suit, black tie, and black shirt grow darker in the shadows.

"Come now, my neglected candle-reader," Gregory cajoles. "All I'm asking is a nod of your bruised and battered head in confirmation. As you can see, another candle-reader among us has already provided the details. And for your simple nod, I think even you will be pleased with the scope of your reward."

After a long pause, Timothy does nod. He has meant all along to keep his candle-read a secret, if just out of spite, but it's obvious now that his father and Gregory have at least one other source. He doesn't know what Gregory is offering for cooperation, but it has been a long time since Timothy has received anything nice.

"Excellent!" Gregory informs.

For a minute, Timothy thinks Gregory will leave without fulfilling his part of the bargain. It's what Timothy's father would do—has done—numerous times in the past.

However, though Gregory does stand and prepare to leave, he doesn't immediately exit through the open glass door. Instead, he walks over to the boy, gently puts a hand to the boy's fingers and easily—though Timothy tries to prevent it—shifts the boy's face to one side. Sympathetically, he shakes his head when he sees the results of Gyle's questioning.

"Quite unexpectedly," Gregory says, "though you may not yet know the how or the why, Timothy, you suddenly have far more power over your father than he has over you. In fact, you have the power to prevent him from ever laying a hand on you again."

"How?" That's definitely a secret Timothy would give a good deal to know. If true, he would gladly candle-read for Gregory until the sun no longer rises.

"From here on out, it's your father who should be afraid of you," Gregory says and is suddenly gone, dissolving into the wind without even bothering, it would seem, to leave the way he entered; although, the floor-to-ceiling glass panel does, quite by itself, somehow loudly bang shut.

#4 TURNABOUT IS FAIR PLAY, ISN'T IT?

Timothy eases out of the corner, slips on a shirt and buttons it shut to pad the bruises on his torso. Walking into the kitchen, he pours himself a bowl of cereal, adding milk from the frig. After sprinkling sugar directly from the sugar bowl over his breakfast, he gets a teaspoon from the utensil drawer, sits at the kitchen table, eats and thinks.

Halfway through, he hears the door to his father's bedroom swing open.

His father's heavy footsteps along the hallway and then in the living room make the floorboards squeak like baby birds in distress.

Timothy doesn't need to look up to know the exact moment his father's menacing body enters the kitchen-to-living-room doorway.

"Your creepy friend Gregory isn't here," Timothy says, carefully spooning another bite of cereal into his sore mouth, commencing chewing with difficulty.

"What do you mean he isn't here?" Gyle growls.

Timothy ignores his father, enjoying Gyle's confusion. Timothy isn't even really sure what's happened.

"Where is he?" Gyle wants to know. His fleeting gaze takes in the whole room, as if Gregory might be lurking somewhere in plain view.

"Gone," Timothy says, in between mouthfuls of cereal. "He slithered out the window through which he slithered in. He did, though, leave a message for you."

"He wouldn't go without telling me," Gyle says, squinting as he cocks his head to the side. "What have you done to him?"

"Me?" Timothy looks up to see the all-too-familiar glare which his father always provides. "Done to him?" Timothy tries to laugh, but his mouth hurts too much. Then he smiles anyway, after realizing the insinuated mockery is more effective. "Gregory seems to me someone who can take care of himself. You, on the other hand…"

"What's that supposed to mean, smart boy?" Gyle asks, raising a hand menacingly as if preparing to strike the boy. By "smart" Gyle insinuates anything but.

Timothy scoops up another spoonful of milky cereal.

"What say you answer my question, or I make you answer it?" Gyle suggests with pure malice.

"Better be careful," Timothy says.

"You're telling *me* to be careful, you little dog turd?"

"Gregory tells you to be careful," Timothy says.

"What nonsense!" Gyle can't believe his ears.

"Seems the times are changing," Timothy says matter-of-factly. "Seems I'm suddenly far more important than I was just a few hours ago, while you…" He leaves the insinuation hanging, knowing that he may well be cutting off his nose to spite his face. Strangely, though, he doesn't feel nearly as frightened of this man, his father, as he always has been before.

"What exactly did Gregory say?" Gyle demands to know.

Timothy, unsure he can remember exactly what Gregory said, delights in the continued confusion and uncertainty on his father's face. Preparing to pretend that Gregory was full of revelations for Timothy to which Gyle hadn't been given one-on-one access, Timothy begins with, "He said if you ever touch me again, you'll be deeply sorry." Seeing the statement effective, Timothy continues more boldly, "He said you'll be held accountable, from here on out, not only by him but by others far more important than he is."

"Bull!" Gyle says, taking two steps forward, only to stop with a suddenness that seems to leave him teetering.

It's the first time Timothy can remember Gyle, double-fisted, starting forward and not finishing the journey.

Timothy rises slowly, trying to read the expression on his father's face. It's one the boy hasn't seen before, and he doesn't have a clue as to how to read it.

"How did you do that?" Gyle points breathlessly.

"Do?" Timothy doesn't have a clue. That is, not until he follows where his father points and sees how the teaspoon in Timothy's hand has gone quite as curly as a corkscrew, allowing the milk-soggy cereal in it to drop into a wet splatter on the tabletop

The lights in the room sputter electrically, and the room quickly darkens.

#5 YOU CALL THIS NORMAL?

The indistinct image solidifies inside the quivering halo of flame. In it, Trish Remoth wishes, more than anything, that she had a normal life and family. Surely, that isn't too much to ask, is it?

Granted, there was a time, before she knew any better, when she found some interest and enjoyment in all the dream stuff and all the weird, candle-gazing hocus-pocus. That said, she was never into it to the degree that her parents and her little sister, Melissa, are.

Trish's dreams are never vivid and seldom come with a remembered story line. Certainly, she's never dreamed anything like Melissa's dream of a blue candle and blue-hooded girl. In fact, Trish's dreams remain so uneventful that her parents, who had initially insisted she tell them everything about them, no longer show any interest in them.

Few of Trish's friends' parents spend long days and nights out in the field, dragging their children along, to look at old rocks and stones. And no way will Trish ever admit to any of her friends that her parents and younger sister, like now, sit around a lit candle, gazing into its flickering flame for a vision. No way at all.

She should be more a part of the family circle. Actually, she has been part of it for almost an hour now. That is, until boredom set in—and not for the first time, either. One thing she's learning about the whole crazy thing: Candle light gives her a headache, and this time is no exception. She said so before, and she said so a few minutes ago. Reluctantly, her parents let her return to the tent they pitched in Dry Wash Gulch. They only ask that Trish return to the circle when her headache gets better.

Well, her headache is better, but she isn't going to go back and sit on the cold dirt and hard stones just to get another headache. Not that she's all that comfortable where she is, but at least she's hunkered down in a cozy, warm, goose-down-filled sleeping bag. What she really wants is to go home.

She's going to miss an important history exam. Her parents provided an excuse, but lied. They said there was a death in the family. What normal parents would purposely have their child miss a test, especially if that child is looking forward to attending a good college and wants, no, *needs*, to maintain an A grade-point average?

Worse, Trish doesn't want to think about missing cheer-leading practice. The squad will call in Georgiana Portland as a substitute. Trish isn't fond of Georgiana. Most likely, Georgiana and her friends, given half the chance, will connive to make the substitution permanent. "Better to have someone who attends all practices than someone who doesn't," Trish can hear Briana James saying to each and every fellow squad member who'll listen.

And what about her boyfriend, Matty? What must he think? Trish's parents refuse to let her call him. Certainly, they aren't keen on her telling him the truth. For whatever the reason, they think it important that,

19

this time around, no one knows where they are. Now, why is that? It's all just too weird for Trish to bear.

Fully clothed in her sleeping bag for padding and extra warmth, Trish struggles to fish out from her pants' pocket her cell phone which she had managed to secrete away. So what that her parents asked her to leave her phone at home? So what that she lied and told them she had done as they asked. After all, they lied, too, didn't they? What kind of an example are they for a young, impressionable girl like her?

She opens her cell phone, surprised by the magnified intensity of its low blue light inside the tent. Fearing the illumination might show from the inside through the canvas, and might bring her parents on the run, she quickly shuts the phone's lid. The shutting sounds surprisingly like a gunshot.

Momentarily frightened, she disappears completely into her bag and reopens her phone there. She pushes the pre-set speed-dial.

Despite all her wishing, Matty doesn't answer immediately. It's still early-morning, after all. His phone is likely under his pillow and set on vibrate, as it always is after official bedtime, so his parents will be less likely to know he's getting a call when he should be sleeping.

"Trish?" he says finally, sleepily, from the other

end. "Where in the heck are you?"

#6 I CANNOT TELL A LIE

Suddenly, Trish doesn't know what to say. She suspects now she should have thought this out, far more, before making the call.

To tell Matty the truth will make Trish's family seem as kooky as they are. To tell him the truth will reveal her parents as liars. To tell him the truth will violate her parents' trust in her, the two having told her clearly not to tell anyone where they were headed, and where they now are.

Not to tell Matty the truth, though, will endanger Trish and his relationship. There is, after all, this promise that both made to each other to never tell the other a lie. Both have seen the disastrous results of lying on other relationships. They're determined not to let it happen to theirs.

"Briana James said your grandmother died," Matty says into the silence.

"Not quite so dire," Trish says, figuring that's the truth, for sure. "It's a family thing. Hopefully, I'll be back in school soon, maybe even tomorrow." If wishes were gold and pigs could fly.

"You're still in town, then?"

"Between Flicker and Seattle," Trish says. She didn't add—out in the scrubland, having hiked in, pitched a tent, and sat around staring at candle flames, trying to figure out some meaning to her little sister's dream of a blue candle and a blue-robed girl. She isn't exactly lying and the details can wait.

"Glad you're okay," Matty says. "Glad your grandmother didn't die. I still miss mine."

"I just don't want you to worry," Trish continues with as much of the truth as she can reveal. "It was all kind of sudden, and I knew you'd wonder what happened."

"You got that right."

"Anyway, I…"

Trish stops talking and listens. She hears something, and not on the phone, but what? Have her parents detected the light in the tent? Have they come to find out what mischief their elder daughter is up to?

"What?" Matty asks from the other end.

"Shhhhhh," Trish insists.

After a minute, she decides she's imagining it all. She doesn't remember Dry Wash Gulch being nearly as creepy the last time around.

"Thought I heard someone," she apologizes. "You know how parents don't like us talking when we should be sleeping—as if we're conspiring to do something they know they'll be dead-set against."

"Don't I, though," Matty says. Why else keep his phone nightly under his pillow, on vibrate?

"So, just don't worry, and I'll be back soon." Certainly, Trish hopes she'll be back soon; she doesn't know how much longer she can take all of this getting-creepier-by-the-minute nonsense. "If there's a delay, I'll call you again." Anyway, she'll *try* to call him again.

"Love you," she says and makes kissing sounds into the phone's mouthpiece, by way of fond farewell.

She breaks their tele-connection before Matty asks or says something that will make Trish tell an out-and-out-lie—or not tell an out-and-out-lie and end up in major hot water as far as her parents are concerned.

She's tucking the phone back into concealment in her pocket, when…she does hear something. And this time, she's certain it's coming from just outside the tent.

Like a turtle, she slides her head out of her sleeping-bag shell and into the darkness held, like her, imprisoned within the enclosing canvas.

She listens.

There is someone or something definitely out there.

"Dad?" she asks. Can she actually see her breath gone misty against the dark, or does she only imagine the air gone icier?

It's as if a punctured bicycle tire is deflating or someone is sniffing or breathing heavily along the tent's perimeter.

"Dad?" she repeats.

"Noooooooooooooooooooo, not dad," comes the hissing, whispered reply.

#7 BY THE LIGHT OF THE SILVERY MOON

Melissa screams non-stop. She continues until her mother slaps her hard across the left side of her face. Then, her screams interrupted by her surprise (her mother never hits her), Melissa begins sobbing uncontrollably.

"No one can help your sister when you're being hysterical," Mary Remoth insists, giving her younger daughter an accompanying shake.

Melissa, though, has been screaming because she's not at all sure *anyone* can help her sister now.

Trish's sleeping bag lay in a jumble outside the tent. Trish quite obviously has been yanked by someone or by something from the discarded bedding. There's hard evidence, by way of scrapes across rock and ground surfaces, that she was dragged into the darkness.

Melissa quiets, and, not sensing her sister anywhere near, fears the worst.

What or who could have done such a thing? How could it or they possibly have managed so quickly? After having heard Trish's cries for help, Melissa and her parents had been at the tent within seconds—only to find Trish gone.

Roger Remoth kneels before a scuffed and dusty rock surface that's punctuated with what he assumes to be his elder daughter's nail marks.

"What is it, Roger?" Mary wants to know.

"Trish's cell phone, I think," Roger says. "I thought she said she left it at home."

"As if we've been the best examples of truth-telling lately," Mary reminds. "And it's gotten us where?"

Roger manipulates the buttons to retrace Trish's last call.

"She talked to Matty," he says.

"Do you think she told him where we are?" Mary wonders aloud.

"Matty wouldn't hurt Trish," Melissa, between sniffles, comes to Matty's defense. "He loves Trish. Trish loves him. They were going to get married."

"Of course," Mary agrees, although she doesn't sound at all convinced of Matty's innocence. "When did Melissa call him?"

"A few minutes ago." Roger reads the call-up information.

"Matty couldn't possibly have gotten here so fast," Melissa continues to argue in the young man's favor.

"Those things can cover an awfully lot of ground in a very short time," Roger says.

"What 'things'?" Melissa wants to know. "What things?" she screams while Roger and Mary stare at each other.

"Calm down, Melissa!" Mary insists. "We'll discuss all this later. Right now, Roger, you'd better phone the police. I suspect our chances of finding our daughter without help are nonexistent."

Roger dials 911. "My daughter has been abducted," he says into the mouthpiece. "We're camped at Dry Wash Gulch."

Melissa hears, but doesn't hear the rest of her father's side of the conversation. She remembers the dark shadow that passed across the candle flame seconds before Trish was abducted. Would Trish be safe now if Melissa had commented upon the event instead of merely assuming her tired eyes had blinked from too much concentration?

"Authorities are on their way," Roger says. "As it

may take some time, do you think we should try, again, to read the candle flame?"

"We've been trying all night," Melissa reminds. "What makes you think we'll come up with something now?" She wishes she didn't remember the shadow passing between her and the light.

"It'll be something to do," Roger says. "We need to do something."

Reluctantly, Melissa returns with her parents to the rocky niche cradling the candle they'd been watching when Trish disappeared.

The wick is extinguished. Did someone brush against it during their attempted rescue of Trish? Did a chance breeze snuff it after they left it, burning, alone?

Mary lights the charred wick and sits, pulling Melissa down beside her. Roger assumes a yoga cross-legged position right angle across the flaming candle from them.

"Try to contact your sister, Melissa," Mary instructs.

"It's not going to work," Melissa says, tears still welling in her eyes. "I know it's not going to work."

"At least try," Mary cajoles. "We've nothing to lose, and what if it does work?"

Melissa straightens her back, breathes in deeply and slowly lets the air out from her lungs as she relaxes her tense muscles and tries her best to concentrate on the innermost part of the flame.

It seems so hopeless. Their whole candle-reading attempt since they arrived at Dry Gulch has been hopeless.

A fleeting ghostly vision of a creature with the claws of a cat, the tail of a snake, and the head and body of a dog suddenly whips into Melissa's line of vision and makes the candle flame momentarily dim and flicker.

As if on cue, somewhere in the very far distance, an unearthly-looking creature raises its head skyward and howls a low and plaintive bay at the moon.

The hairs along Melissa's neck stand on end.

#8 HISSING STONES

Naked to the point of discarding even his flashlight, Johnny-Three-Spirits pushes back the buffalo-hide flap covering the opening of the traditional sweat lodge and steps in.

The wall of heat hits him like a battle axe, leaving him momentarily breathless.

He shuts his eyes to adjust to the darkness. When he opens them, he still can't see, and it's only because he knows the space around him that he's able to find his preassigned place and sit.

Across from him, there's a loud hiss, frightening him, why? He knows it's only his grandfather, Jimmy-Who-Knows, ladling water onto hot stones. As proof, another wave of water-laden heat strikes him and wraps around him like a hot blanket. His pores open and sweat begins streaming down his face and body.

"Is it done?" Jimmy-Who-Knows asks his grandson.

"Yes, grandfather."

"And were there…problems?"

"It was a difficult struggle but, this time, I kept wolf dominant."

"Did the girl, Trish, at any time see you?"

"Only for a moment. Wolf made her faint."

Johnny senses, more than sees, his grandfather's disappointed head shake.

"From concealment at a distance, I watched her recover," Johnny adds.

"That much at least is reason for encouragement."

"I am sorry, grandfather," Johnny apologizes. "I was unable to control the shifts. It was like in the very beginning, all four battling for control. I hadn't a clue that I fetched Trish, not Melissa, for you."

"You say you bit her just outside Dry Wash

Gulch?"

"Yes, grandfather. I couldn't help myself. As I said, it was as if your teachings to me had never been taught."

"You say it was done as serpent. Did you deliver venom?"

"I tried not to, but I may have failed. I wrestled so hard to get back to speedier wolf that I was distracted."

"We must monitor her very carefully. Should she, as a result, become one of us, she will need help with the transition. That would, of course, be your responsibility, if, indeed, it happens. In that case, you must be her initiator and help her find her way as a shape-shifter, even as I have been your guide."

"Yes, grandfather."

"And now, let's try once again to more fully understand the situation."

"I tried on my own without success."

"I suspect this is because we are on the verge of events long prophesied, that we, over the centuries, have denied will ever come."

"The battle after the floods, you mean?"

"All signs seem to say so. I would know better, had we accessed the right girl—even briefly. Unfortunately, Trish already verges on too old; and I am way too old. If the time is near, it will be for you and

Melissa, the young ones, to bear the responsibility of saving yourselves as well as the rest of us."

"Is there some other way besides Melissa?"

"We can risk a *koh-no-toh-ka*—a chant-to-see-the-future. As you know, there is great danger in that, and even then, it may not work."

"We need to know—I need to know—if just to prepare, grandfather."

"Then, let us chant—together—here—now."

Jimmy-Who-Knows ladles yet more water onto the hot stones. The sizzling and wall of heat strike Johnny-Three-Spirits and his grandfather, awakening that within them which they seek.

Without willing it, and unable to control it, Johnny's body becomes serpent, swiftly gliding across the floor to enwrap and entrap his grandfather in a suffocating embrace.

#9 DISTANCES TRAVELED

Cooper Loor senses that it's time to officially start his day.

Actually, his last name is Loo, not Loor, but he changed to the latter—first with his schools' (and there had been many) and later his mother's permission. His mother completed the process, winning his father over after three years of Cooper suffering non-stop taunting in the various schools, "Hey, Cooper Pooper." Cooper was always amazed by how quickly school children, world-wide, picked up his last name being the British word for toilet, and even more so using it when any opportunity appeared to humiliate him in front of anyone to whom he felt any semblance of closeness. It was utterly intolerable.

Originally, Madison Loo argued that the schoolyard bullying would merely help his son build "character." Madison felt himself a better man for his early-on having had the gumption, fortitude and physique to defend himself in such adversity. He wore the word Loo proudly on the nameplates of his crisp military uniforms, his desk, and his door. As a lieutenant colonel in the United States Air Force, he no longer heard the derogatory chants that were still performed too far behind his back for him to notice.

In time, because Madison loved his wife and his son, the latter a poor specimen of the man Lt. Col. Loo had become, he acquiesced, but only, he pointed out, temporarily.

Four assignments at different bases around the United States later, Cooper, now a teenager blossoming into a stellar example of physical fitness and a powerhouse to be reckoned with in high-school sports, still keeps the "r" on the end of his last name. His reasoning is that it's become a preventative from his having to beat the crap out of all of his wise-ass fellow schoolmates; most of whom he rightly figures he can, at this point, dominate in any fair bout of fisticuffs.

Cooper stretches his muscular right arm from beneath the warm comforter. His large, easily-can-palm-a-basketball right hand slaps the alarm button before the wail of the morning alarm can interrupt the quiet of the morning.

He gets up, showers, dresses, and heads downstairs to the kitchen, along the way passing his parents' room. His mother is sleeping, alone, in a big king-sized bed.

Cooper's father called last night to say that circumstances would keep him at the Air Force base for the night. After assuring his wife that the incident wouldn't cause him to renege on his promise of spending more time with the family, he explained that it will take him time to settle in as official military liaison between Rockpoint Air Force Base and the expanding town of Flicker. There is a lot he has to quickly catch up on.

The relationship between the Rockpoint Air Force Base and town isn't good. When Flicker was merely a wide spot in the road, the adjoining air base was isolated in the center of a wide stretch of central Washington State wilderness. Since the extensive underground water system had been discovered, two new housing projects nearing completion and two more on the drawing boards are beginning to encroach. Even a Wal-Mart is insinuated in Flicker's future.

Whatever it was that originally prompted the government to build its air-force base smack-dab in the middle of once-desolate scrublands—and Cooper doesn't have a clue—it is obviously making his father and Lt. Col. Loo's military superiors nervous to have the immediately adjoining area suddenly filling up with civilians.

That, though, is his father's problem. Cooper's concern for the moment is getting himself breakfast. The rest of the day he'll spend trying to fit into yet another school that has its own well-established groups and cliques and social clubs. Luckily, Cooper's expertise at fitting in has grown like his body.

Turning toward the refrigerator, Cooper glances through the kitchen window at the bleak vista desiccating in the sun before his eyes despite the incredible amount of water said to be located underground. To Cooper it's all just a vast expanse of wasteland extending to the horizon.

His view and musings, however, are brought short by the sight of an apparently unconscious and disheveled Trish Remoth sprawled unceremoniously on his family's shriveled excuse of a lawn.

#10 MORE CREATURES THAN A ZOO

Within the flame, one image in particular surges to take on a life of its own. "Oh, Mom, please, no!" Melissa Remoth is saying, her accompanying groan low, loud, and punctuated with frustration.

Back in their home, her mother, Mary, has returned with a third candle during the last hour, still desperate to have Melissa divine some hint as to Trish's whereabouts. This candle is bright yellow and smells of freshly-squeezed lemon. Even the police helicopter that just finished infra-red scanning the Dry Wash Gulch camp area hasn't been able to find Trish's heat signature. Which means what? Trish is either stone-dead cold, or has been taken away, where?

"None of these candles are working," Melissa, tired, insists grumpily, doubting they'll ever let her sleep again. "We're wasting our time."

"Don't say that!" Mary chides her daughter. "If the candles aren't working, it's because it's the wrong combination of candles—and you. Your father, Trish, and my candle-powers have been in decline for quite some time. We all know that."

"But are mine really on the rise, as you keep suggesting? It doesn't seem so."

"Did you, or did you not envision the chimera while candle-reading at Dry Wash Gulch?"

"Chimera? Do you mean that part cat, snake, and dog creature? Do you actually think a thing like that exists?"

Mary places the candle on the table. She lights the candle wick, then pulls out a chair into which she gently insists her younger daughter sit.

"You tell me," she says. "There are people who still don't believe vampires exist—or werewolves, or witches, or warlocks, or candle-readers. You and I, though, know that they all do. So, just because we've never seen a tangible flesh and blood chimera doesn't mean that one or more isn't out there—somewhere now —with your sister. You need merely ask the candle and wait patiently for its answer in the flame."

Melissa pauses, collects her thoughts, leans forward and, to her mother's surprise, blows out the candle flame. Inadvertently (or, is it on purpose?) she inhales the twisting thread of smoke. She doesn't, however, cough, though her eyes seem to glaze over.

"No need to ask," she says in an other-worldly voice as she turns to her mother. "Know that chimeras exist. Know that we shall one day soon, to our peril, have to deal with one. Know that this time, though, it isn't a chimera but a shape-shifter, and one who doesn't have any more answers to what is going on than we do, but is seeking them as frantically as we are."

The telephone rings and Mary and Roger, in the background, are so taken back by what their daughter has just told them, they seem unable to register that the phone is beckoning them.

The phone rings again.

"A shape-shifter," Roger echoes and nods over the possible likelihood. "Why didn't you or I think of that, Mary?"

The phone rings again.

"We didn't think of it, my dear, because we're quickly being excluded from a game we're too old to play."

The phone rings again.

"You should answer it," Melissa says in the same haunting voice as before. "The authorities want to tell us they've found Trish; though they don't know it's only because the shape-shifter has purposely dropped her there."

#11 ONCE BITTEN

"Thank God!" Roger Remoth says into the telephone mouthpiece. "Is she really okay?... You found her where?... Does she know who abducted her?... Yes, of course, I understand." He checks his wristwatch. "We can be there within the hour... Thank you, and please tell our daughter we're on our way." He hangs up and says to his wife and his younger daughter, "They found Trish across town on the lawn of one of the tract houses allocated to air-force personnel."

"To have transported her so far, so fast, the shape-shifter would have had to be a large four-legged animal," Melissa says.

"Is Trish okay?" Mary anxiously asks her husband.

"According to the police, she's rambling incoherently," Roger says. "They say she's babbling about being abducted by a wolf, a snake, and a cougar. The police are assuming she's suffering the aftereffects of being drugged. They think they've located the two syringe puncture wounds."

"The shape-shifter, as snake, bit her," Melissa says; it isn't a question. "Neither police nor doctor will recognize it as a snake bite; the punctures are too far apart for any snake they know. The larger the shape-shifter, the larger the snake. The larger the snake, the larger the bite."

"They're taking her to the hospital, assuming likely rape."

"Oh, dear God, tell me she wasn't raped," Mary begs.

"She says not, but the police say they have to be sure. They'll run a toxicology screen, as well."

"Melissa," Mary turns to her daughter, "please tell me your sister wasn't raped."

Melissa shrugs and shakes her head. "I don't know. I only know that if there is any poison in her, whatever it may be, we'll need to watch her closely. As will the shape-shifter. He'll want to either help or control her, if he's turned her, won't he? So, everyone should be on guard for someone—anyone—more curious about her than usual. Which might prove difficult once it gets around she's been kidnapped, given local curiosity. I would think the shape-shifter would most likely be a young, local, Native American —maybe a classmate who knows her. Then, again, it could be someone older, from outside, with more sinister intentions."

"Can't you be more specific?" her father presses.

"I sense that he bit her by mistake."

"He?" Mary wants the gender confirmed.

"I think so. Also, I think, like I've already said, that his intent was merely to find answers. That would have best been achieved by wolf or cougar quickly and hurriedly carrying Trish out of the area. That he lingered, even bothering with snake, let alone with a snake bite, says incomplete control. Someone grown old or feeble, his powers not what they once were; more likely, someone young, his powers not yet fully realized. Someone old or young with powers waxing or waning because of whatever is happening all around us."

"Is he friend or enemy?" Roger asks.

"We really should get to the hospital, Roger," Mary interrupts. "The police and Trish will be wondering what's holding us up."

"I feel the presence of many friends, many enemies," Melissa says, her gaze returning to the still-smoldering candle, "but I can't, at least at the moment, identify any of them," she adds with a tired sigh.

"We have to go," Mary insists and heads for the door. In the car together, pulling out of the driveway, Melissa puts a hand to her forehead and winces, adding further, "I can also tell you that there are many more— friends and enemies, beasts and beasties—all determined to get here."

#12 THE STAY-AT-HOME

"Timothy!"

No doubt about it. His father's voice still sends chills up and down the teenager's spine that literally make the young man shiver. Timothy assumes it will take time for that reflex action to cease and desist. He's determined, though, that it will.

"Timothy!"

Timothy wills himself to stretch and press the increase volume button on the kitchen television's remote control.

The local morning news, now loud enough to drown his father's calls, is devoted to the abduction and recovery of Timothy's classmate, Trish Remoth. Her assailant is thought to be serially a pervert... a madman... a druggie—maybe, even, a cult of druggies —or, when you come right down to it, no one is really sure; not even, it seems, Trish Remoth.

"Timothy!" His father's voice rises above the din of the news.

The joy of momentarily levitating a morning-breakfast PopTart from within the toaster almost cancels that last shout from the bedroom, down the hall, across the living room and kitchen, to where Timothy is sitting.

PopTart eaten, glass of milk drunk, Timothy fills a quart jar with tap water, grabs a box of cereal from the countertop and walks slowly towards and into his father's room.

"About damned time!" Gyle Gril accuses his son from the bed.

Timothy avoids his father's reach, placing the quart of water on a bedside nightstand.

"What's the problem?" Timothy asks. "School bus will be here any minute."

"What do you mean, what's the bloody problem?" Gyle accuses.

Timothy steps back to admire the way his father is locked in by the bed's metal frame, bent up and over, securing the man's body ever-so tightly to the mattress.

"I'm afraid this will have to wait until I get back from school," Timothy says nonchalantly. "In the meantime, here's something to eat." He tosses the box of cereal onto the bed. Some of the box contents spill, looking like bugs scattering among the rumpled blankets and sheets.

"Gregory won't like this," his father warns.

"Gregory is even older than you are. If he wants to keep in the game that's being played, he will have to learn to rely on young people like me. I thought he made that perfectly clear the other night."

Timothy leaves his fettered father and catches the school bus.

On board, Jack Plenoc takes the seat next to him.

"Suppose you heard about Trish Remoth?" Jack half-says, half-asks.

"Is there anyone in Flicker who hasn't?"

"I hear she was raped," Jack whispers eagerly behind the back of his hand.

"I heard she wasn't," Timothy replies matter-of-factly, inwardly annoyed by the jackass sitting next to him.

At school, Timothy looks for Melissa Remoth. It's hard to find her in the new, larger, building complex. Within the last year, the student body's more than doubled.

Expecting to find her in the center of a crowd of curiosity-seekers all asking about her sister, he's surprised to find her standing alone in front of her locker.

"Melissa," he says kindly—if not exactly on intimate speaking terms, they've at least shared classes together. He finds her surprisingly cute, despite the saddened, tired eyes she turns towards him. Before, his whole world centered on his father, and he didn't have time to notice girls.

"Timothy," she says. "Gril, right?"

"Can we talk for a minute?"

She checks her wristwatch. "I'm afraid I can't tell you anything more about what happened to my sister than what you've already heard on the news."

"Actually, it's not your sister I want to talk to you about, but a certain girl in blue with a blue candle."

Melissa is surprised but not nearly as surprised as Timothy expects. She tilts her head slightly to one side. Her pretty blue eyes narrow to get a better look at him.

"Why is it, I wonder," she says, "that I thought you'd be Native American?"

#13 NONE OF YOUR BEES-WAX!

The flame wavers, sputters, and for a brief instant dies almost to nothingness. Pitch black. Black. Dark grey. Grey. Clotted cream. Pale white. White. "Ohhhhhhhhh." The latter hurts his eyes.

"It's all right," a low, masculine voice reassures him.

Maybe, but Johnny-Three-Spirits doesn't feel all right, although he is encouraged. "Grandfather, is that you? I thought I'd killed you."

"Yes, I'm here, for awhile thinking you *had* killed me. As it turns out, though, I'm alive and well, and possibly more enlightened from the near-death experience."

"Where are we?" Not the sweat lodge, unless the rocks are cooled, the heat's gone, and electric lights have been installed.

"Back at my house."

"You carried me here?"

"Actually, it would seem you carried me, and then collapsed."

"I'm sorry. I lost control—again."

"Not as badly as the last time. Last time, you were snake, and cougar, and wolf. Last time, you bit Melissa Remoth. This time, you were only snake and didn't bite grandfather. Progress. So we shall say until proven otherwise."

"What keeps happening that so pushes things so out of whack?"

"A question which obviously requires yet more searching."

"Did chant-to-see-the-future tell us nothing, then?"

"Snake interrupted the chant. In afterthought, I'm thinking we need call on something more insightful than a chant."

"Such a thing exists?"

"If I can still believe my dreams."

"You had a dream?"

"If dream is what occurs while losing consciousness from the life-sucking squeeze of a form-changer-grandson as snake."

"And what did you dream?"

"Of you and I, scooping up warm wax from angry scrubland bees. Of you and I, working the wax to make it malleable. Of you and I, rolling it into a waxy column of crusty gold and creamy fragmented honeycombs... with wick."

"A candle?"

"So it would seem."

"Have you become a candle-reader, then, between sweat lodge and now?"

"No. Have you?"

"Not that I'm aware. And for as long as I can remember, I have heard you and the other elders say that our people have been deprived of one for more than three generations. Which was why we set out to snatch Melissa Remoth to know her latest reading, yes?"

"And possibly why, in my dream, grandson, Melissa is with us to do the reading."

"Unless, of course, I spoil things by snatching her sister instead of her again."

#14 A DIVINE FRIENDSHIP

"Okay, Michaels, turn loose and let the kid up!"

Sydney Michaels does as Coach Waynright instructs, releasing his opponent from the head-lock.

Both sweaty young wrestlers scamper to their feet.

"Shower, Michaels," coach says. "Loor, you stick around for a minute."

Sydney Michaels does again as instructed and heads for the locker room. Coach Waynright waits patiently, arms folded, until Sydney disappears into the locker-room access corridor on the far side of the gym.

"You should have seen that takedown coming from a mile away, buddy," the coach tells Cooper. "You're rusty as hell and I need someone up to my standards."

"I'm good at playing catch-up, coach," Cooper promises. "I just need time to get back into regular workouts now that my dad's military transfer here is complete."

"I'm not saying you can't be brought up to speed," coach says. "In fact, I'm actually impressed by what I see. That said, later today, I've a couple more kids trying out for this one available slot. I'll take a look at them and have my final decision to all three of you by first-period tomorrow."

"That's fair, coach," says Cooper.

"So, go shower... and don't be late for your next class: you have to maintain the grade-point in order to play in any kind of ongoing extracurricular sport here at Flicker High. I can't tell you how many good athletes I've had to let go because they thought brawn was all they needed on a wrestling mat."

Coach Waynright nods toward the locker-room-access corridor, turns, and heads in another direction for the weight room.

Cooper peels off his sweaty T-shirt in the corridor. At his locker, he discards his sweaty shoes, sweaty athletic socks, sweaty shorts, and sweaty jockstrap, picking up a fresh towel from the convenient wire basket always stuffed full of them, and wraps his sweaty neck in the warm, soft terry-cloth.

In the shower room, Sydney Michaels is already showering down the way. Cooper turns to the plumbing just inside the doorway, hangs his towel on the pipes, and reaches for the water release.

"Hey, Loors, get your studly ass over here," Sydney yells and pats the wall tiles of the shower space immediately beside his. "You and I have some talking to do, and I don't feel like screaming."

Cooper retrieves his towel and walks the distance

next to where Sydney is ducking his head under the misting spray.

For not the first time, Cooper's impressed by Sydney's physique, tanned, and now made sensuously glossy by soap-slick water. He wonders if his classmate came by his great body naturally, because of good genes, or if he, like Cooper, has had to spend long hours bulking up. Intuition tells him it's a combination of both.

Cooper re-hangs his towel, turns on the water, steps into it.

"Listen: You ever again hand me a takedown on a silver platter, and I'm going to beat the living crap out of you," Sydney says, sounding like he means it. "I don't need hand-outs to pin your sorry ass to any mat."

"Actually, I didn't hand you anything," Cooper says. He reaches for the soap and begins lathering his tightly-muscled chest and belly. "I've been off my regular training regimen, that's all. Although, I can see where you might think the new kid on the block is out to brown-nose Mr. Popularity in order to gain social acceptance."

"Obviously, you have me confused with my older brother. He's the one you should be kissing up to if you want social acceptance around here."

"Nah, he's too unapproachable. Besides, he's

obviously fond of you and includes you in just about everything. It's often easier for a wannabe like me to try the backdoor approach."

Sydney laughs. It's a nice laugh; low-key and genuine.

"Obviously, you did your homework and know I'm gay," he says, turning in the spray to face, more directly, his possibly soon-to-be teammate.

"Yeah, I know you're gay, and I also know you're the ward of a vampire." Sydney's attractively square jaw drops. "And I..." The soapy index finger of Cooper's right hand reaches out and almost, but not quite, touches down on the deep indent at the base of Sydney's throat; it slowly air-traces a line down the middle of the young man's chest to Sydney's slightly innie navel. "...am a diviner who divines that you and I are going to quickly become the best of friends."

#15 SISTERS, OR NOT

Uxana Uxl is young, afraid, and cold. She can do nothing about her age. She can do nothing about her fear. Unsuccessfully, she tries to make herself warmer by pulling the blue cloak even more tightly around her. The last large candle, blue as Uxana's smaller candle had been blue, scorches the darkness, providing flickering light but little warmth.

Uxana could get warmer simply by walking down the long, rocky corridor into the sunlight entering the narrow mouth of the cave perched over the perilous drop-off, but she can't spare the time. Too much time has already elapsed. She has to monitor closely this latest burn-down—that of her mentor Zila Bwl—and maybe others of The Sisterhood. She has to be here to do what she can do, should anything more go wrong.

She should have known when she asked the girl, "How long?" and the apparition hadn't a clue that the time lapse was already too long. It was now clear from how, one after another, three of the all-important four larger candles sloughed all their wax, without results. All three are now merely lifeless splotches on the black basalt floor. The smaller candles, still in the pile, are probably—fatally, Uxana wonders? —contaminated, too: burrowed by long-dead bugs, made brittle or crumbly from age, split and cracked when the natural temperature regulator had malfunctioned—how long ago was anyone's guess.

Uxana is sorely afraid her candle, similar in color to the larger one of her mentor that is burning now, might have been the only one, large or small, to functionally survive. Why else had her wick spontaneously combusted when she was fifth in the pre-planned revival sequence of large red, large yellow, large green, large blue, then Uxana's smaller blue? Granted, one such anomaly of sequence had occurred after the first flood, but such an event had never recurred since.

She leans back against the hard stone and trembles, but not just from the continuing chill. Energy pulses all about her, like small electric arcs, more powerful than any she's ever known here. Another purging by flood water must surely be imminent. Her thoughts turn to how she, on her own, can vacate everyone from the area in preparation for another soon-to-happen deluge.

She tries again to mind-contact the apparition. Even if it has no answer, she concludes it might be an indication of people somewhere near, maybe even within the flood zone. Likely, some mortals who have accidently wandered in; there have been no warnings since the last flood. Maybe some mortals with psyches genetically attuned to the massive power surges that are apparently building, building. Newbies with remnant DNA from times before their ancestors chose mortality over Magic?

Unfortunately, Uxana's skills at summoning are insufficiently honed, as they were before having gone candle with the last flood. Even with the extra benefit of the Magic-boosting emanations already registering off-scale in intensity, no visions come. Meaning, of course, that the girl-apparition had most likely revived before Uxana, and that the retrieving had stripped her mentor and everyone else ahead of Uxana of their powers. Who in The Sisterhood could have done such a wicked and perverse, not to mention incredibly dangerous, thing? Besides, Uxana didn't recognize the apparition other than that she appeared to be a pretty thing.

So, had Magic suddenly reverted to mortals, leaving everyone else including Uxana's kind suddenly out of the picture? If so, it wasn't a pretty scenario. The Magic of this place had never been something in which novices could safely dabble.

Her eyelids grow heavy. How strange that she should desire sleep, having slept so long. She immediately begins the mental exercises long-ago prescribed to keep those of The Sisterhood alert.

"Ooooooooooooooooo," comes a mournful moan from within the flickering darkness.

The lit candle wick flares, briefly and brightly, and then, as if pinched by ghostly fingertips, goes out.

#16 THE BOYFRIEND

Midday. Roger Remoth knocks, then at her call, opens the door to his older daughter's bedroom and stands hesitant in the breach.

"Someone here to see you," he says with a disapproving frown, stepping back to let Matty Donnelly push awkwardly past him into the room.

"Hi, babe!" Matty says, joining Trish who's cross-legged on her bed. He smiles by way of additional greeting.

"Hi, back to you," she says, glad to see him, keenly aware of the way his smile lights up a room. Both his cheeks dimple. Little creases form at the corners of his light blue eyes. The cleft in his chin sinks deeper, enhancing his strongly masculine presence.

"Don't make this overly long, Trish," her father says. "You need your rest." Roger leaves, purposefully not closing the door behind him.

"I don't think your father likes me much," Matty says. He pauses long enough to deliver a quick kiss to Trish's forehead. His blond hair smells pleasantly of the desert around Flicker. He moves to the visitor's chair, bedside.

"What daddy doesn't like is that I called you on the cell phone. I'd promised him I wouldn't take it with me to Dry Wash Gulch. Then, I'd no sooner hung up from talking when I was kidnapped."

"He doesn't think I told anyone where you were, does he?"

"He doesn't know what to think, Matty. Besides, you really didn't know where I was, did you?"

"What in the heck were you doing, anyway?" Matty has been wondering ever since he heard.

"You know how my parents have this thing for rocks." Trish has thought about and amply rehearsed what to tell him. Most importantly, it isn't exactly a lie. "They think Melissa and I should love them, too. They hear of something geologically interesting, and they figure we should all go, as a family, usually immediately, to see it. You figure."

"The police have any clues?"

"Not that they're saying."

"You remember anything more?"

"A snake. A cat. A dog. Maybe, even, an Indian."

"An Indian? Like a surround-the-wagons-we're-being-attacked-by-Indians type?"

"Yeah, but don't tell anyone, because that part is really vague. As is the part about the number 'three'."

"Three? As in Three Blind Mice? Three Little Pigs? Three kidnappers?"

"Whatever, whoever, maybe nothing, it's probably

just a left-over hallucination."

"I heard the bastard drugged you."

"You heard wrong. I got stuck with a needle or needles. Twice. No sign that anything was injected though. The police say some sadistic perverts get off on weird things like that."

Mary Remoth appears with a vase of red roses.

"From Matty," she tells Trish. "I've put them in water. They'll have you thinking of him until he comes back the next time. Right now, you need to get some rest."

"All I've been doing is resting."

"I'll come back tomorrow, babe," Matty says, standing. He kisses her on the cheek. "Promise."

Matty leaves. Heading down the front walk, he can feel Mr. Remoth's gaze through the house's front picture window nailing him to the paving stones.

"Hey, buddy!" someone calls from across the street.

Matty glances over to see Sydney Michaels and the new kid, Cooper—Cooper something—and heads in their direction.

"Your girlfriend up to visitors?" Sydney asks. "Some of the kids at school would like to stop by."

"Probably best for everyone to wait for a couple more days," Matty decides. Mr. Remoth isn't welcoming, but, then, that might be special treatment just for Matty.

"You know Cooper, here, don't you? Soon to be joining us on the wrestling team."

"Actually, Coach Waynright isn't going to decide until tomorrow," Cooper reminds.

"I've seen a couple of the other guys up for the slot," Matty says. "Joey Spellman pinned each of them to the mat in thirty seconds. You've no competition from that direction."

"So, how is Trish really doing?" Sydney probes.

"As well as anyone kidnapped, poked with a needle or needles, and still trying to deal with the aftermath of hallucinations about a snake, a cat, and a dog." He almost adds—and about a Native American, and the number three.

"She'll be okay," Cooper assures.

"If that's true, you know more about it than the quack-quack doctors do," Matty says.

"Maybe that's because Cooper, here, is a bona-fide diviner, buddy," Sydney informs.

"Isn't that someone who goes around with a forked stick, looking to find water?"

"Come to think of it..." Sidney looks askance at Cooper. "Not in this case, though. Cooper divines the future. Go ahead, Cooper, tell Matty something that's going to happen to him."

"My insights aren't all that automatic, if you know what I mean," Cooper excuses.

"Ah, come on!" Sydney insists. "At least try."

"Sure, go ahead." Matty challenges, finding the whole thing difficult to believe, though his interest is piqued.

Cooper bows his face into the fold formed by his two open hands.

"Do...do...do...do," Sydney chants the theme song from a popular scary TV show.

Cooper opens his fingers, anchoring them, claw-like, to his face. "You're destined to have a close encounter of the third kind with a werewolf," he informs Matty.

"No shit, Sherlock?" Sydney responds.

Matty's eyes squint. His lips purse. He looks from Sydney to Cooper. He bursts into full-throated laughter. "Damn!" he chides and gives Sydney's left bicep a quick and forceful fist-jab. "What's up with the two of you, trying to take me for a bloody idiot like that?"

#17 CANDLE IN THE WIND

It's dark as Timothy mounts the front steps of his

house. He hasn't been doing anything in particular to be out so late—he's just been out to be out, enjoying the freedom he's never known before. Timothy's new independence feels good but strange. It will, likely, take him awhile, but he's already certain he'll get used to it.

He unlocks the door and steps inside. He shuts the door behind him and leans his back against it. He doesn't turn on the houselights. Instead, he slowly scans the darkness of the living-room in front of him, listening for sounds above and beyond those the house makes on its own. He sniffs the air. Something smells foul. That's new since he left.

"Are you going to say hello," he asks finally, "or are you still hoping to jump out and scare the bejezus out of me?"

"Aren't you the killjoy!" comes the response. A black candle suddenly flares on one end of the far window sill. There's the accompanying smell of tar (and brimstone?).

The flickering candlelight unveils the darker shadow of Gregory Ranlin parenthesized within the shadows of the room.

"I was, indeed, hoping to give you a little, 'Boo!'" Gregory admits. "I suppose I should have known you'd expect me, with your powers so quickly on the rise. Certainly, enough to keep your dear dad locked in one place for awhile."

"You've sucked dad's blood so often and for so long, I figured his cries for help would likely disturb your sleep."

"Ah, so many people crying for help these days. I long-ago learned to tune them out. Most of them, anyway. However, when he was still so distraught after nightfall..."

"Speaking of the old man, shouldn't we join him?"

"Actually, I prefer him where you left him, much to his chagrin. Although you might consider, next time, providing a bed pan, as without one, you've his mess to clean up."

"He has his mess to clean up, you mean."

"Are you wondering already if and when your powers will surpass even mine?"

"No denying that thought crossed my mind."

"Best to remember that I've been around for a very, *very* long time. Even with my powers admittedly on the wane, I've a few tricks up my sleeve that could still catch you unaware."

"That's why I've decided to work with you. I am now able to tell you that the Remoth candle-readers know no more about why Trish Remoth was kidnapped than you do, except to suspect that the deed was done

by a Native American shape-shifter who was digging
for information, also. Demons, just as curious as you, it
would seem, are standing in a long line to find the
meaning of this envisioned girl in blue with her blue
candle."

"And you came upon this information, how?
Candle-reading, were you?"

"No, simply by asking. Sometimes a direct
approach is the best. Anyway, Melissa Remoth seems to
think so. In fact, I think she's rather taken with me."

"An increased power of seduction among those of
you being mysteriously force-fed?"

"I certainly hope so. I've a lot of catching up to
do."

"I'm thinking you should do your catching up at
my place, Timothy, where I can keep a better and a
closer watch on you. Think you'd like that? Moving out
of this dump, away from your abusive father, into that
big, beautiful, old house of mine, where you'll have
long days in which to get into to all kinds of mischief
with my other two wards?"

"What would my father do without his punching
bag?"

"Let me worry about your father. In fact..."
Gregory levitates to a window sill and opens the
window with a flick of his fingers. "Come, this very

second. Hop on up here with me. We'll go settle you in
to your new digs. I'll come back later and pacify your
daddy dear."

Timothy takes two steps forward, then pauses.

"No need to be fearful, Timothy," Gregory
encourages. "I fed before you arrived. Your father, as
usual, was most obliging, although less so than usual."

"Possibly, though, you might be thinking of...
dessert?"

Gregory laughs, showing his fanged teeth,
brilliantly white in the darkness, illuminated only by the
one flickering flame.

"I do so love a sense of humor," Gregory says.
"Humor's so damned hard to come by, these days. Most
blood, though, as you may one day be lucky enough to
discover, is blood is blood is blood." His right hand
extends. His right index finger flexes in invitation.
"Come on, now. Over and up. Even I'm beginning to
tire of your father's stench."

With Gregory's assistance, Timothy joins the
handsome vampire on the window sill.

"Face me and take hold of both my wrists,"
Gregory instructs. "Hold tightly."

Timothy does as instructed.

"Information sources are so much more difficult
to come by than food," Gregory says. "There are so

many people able to plot mischief in the light of day, while I'm relegated only to the dark of the night."

Suddenly, they both disappear. The wind into which they've been sucked back-blows into the room, fluttering one of the curtains into the candle flame where the material ignites with a loud and ominous POOF!

#18 JOCK BONDING

"How about we take a closer look?" Sydney suggests.

"Don't you think you might at least want to give me flowers and a box of chocolates first?" Cooper says.

"Very funny," Sydney grants, flashing a wide smile of appreciation. "Come on."

He tosses Cooper another bag of natural almonds and heads for the stairs. Cooper follows.

"You're sure Ranlin isn't going to mind?"

"The first thing Mr. Ranlin is going to suggest, when you two meet up, is that you call him Gregory. As for his minding... he probably would if the telescope wasn't pre-set. As it is, it's just a case of my pushing a button, and you putting an eye to the eyepiece. How easy is that not to screw up?"

"I wouldn't want him angry."

"Angry enough to bite your studly neck, and bleed you dry, you mean? Don't worry. Gregory is up and out so early this evening, he'll come back full as a tick. Of course, without my having told, you wouldn't even be able to tell that he's not just another friendly, charming human being. Besides, when he finds out you're a diviner, he's going to want you up and about in sunlight, not hampered by forever being in the dark. Which reminds me... did you really see a werewolf in Matty Donnelly's future?"

"As I've said, what I see isn't usually all that clear. This time was no exception. It's like a slideshow gone hyper-warp. Whatever I saw, as regards Matty, though, definitely looked lupine."

"Lupine?"

"Wolf-like. Hirsute."

"Hirsute?"

"Hairy."

"Jeez, why don't you just say so? Obviously, you haven't attended school in Flicker your whole life. Here, even one-syllable words get us jocks all confused."

"A slight exaggeration, I would guess."

"Okay, but not by much; believe me. Just remember that if you want to come across as a genuine

Flicker High jock, keep your conversation down to a few barely decipherable grunts."

"I thought Coach Waynright said scholastics count."

"Coach Waynright says a lot of things that aren't true. I'll bet, if confronted, he'd even deny that he likes watching us boys naked in the shower."

"Does he? I mean, like watching us boys naked in the shower?"

"Don't worry, buddy, it never goes any farther than a gawk and sigh of jealous envy. The coach is harmless. I, on the other hand..."

On the second-floor landing, they take a skywalk to the observatory out back. From the road out front, few people would guess the large Tudor mansion comes complete with the most extensive sky-observing equipment this side of the astronomy department at the University of Washington, Seattle. Nor that the house's owner has not only discovered a comet, Gregorran 6, but is published in several prestigious scientific journals, and is widely respected by heavens-watching peers.

"To prove how concerned Gregory is—not—about any of us accessing his precious telescope, please note..." Sydney tries the observatory door, and it opens. "...that he doesn't even bother to lock the place up. Try getting into his bedroom, though, especially after dawn, and you'll need a wrecking ball and box of dynamite."

"He sleeps in a regular bedroom, then? Not in a coffin or grave? Surely, at least a coffin?"

"Haven't a clue. I can only tell you for sure that he goes into his bedroom just before dawn, every morning, and shuts the door. I've been in there, during the night, and I've seen no coffin. A big bed. A lot of windows. Drapes not nearly heavy enough—my personal opinion—I mean, if it's true that daylight for him is a killer."

"You think it may not be?"

"I only know that he keeps insisting that a whole lot of what people believe about vampires just isn't so. He even insinuated, once, that a silver bullet wouldn't kill him."

"Isn't that what kills a werewolf?"

"I don't know. Maybe we should ask Matty?" Sydney laughs. Cooper laughs nervously, too. "This way," Sydney says. "I want to show you the great view from the observation deck at the top of the dome. On clear days, you can see all of the way to Dry Falls."

The two maneuver a series of ascending metal staircases and an eventual narrow metal catwalk that dead-ends at a metal door.

Sydney pushes open the door and steps on out.

Cooper follows.

"Say, whose house do you think is burning down to the ground over there?" Sydney asks, pointing.

#19 DO YOU SEE WHAT I SEE?

"Zila? Is that you?" Uxana asks the darkness.

"I'm weak," comes the distant reply. "I can't see. What is this?"

"Rejuvenation malfunctions," Uxana says, hoping against hope that her mentor, once revived, will have some answers. She's not encouraged by the fade-in, fade-out, quality of her Big Sister's voice.

After a moment, "Who are you?" Zila asks.

"Uxana."

"Uxana Uxl? Have the others already rejuvenated?"

"So far, we're the only two."

"The only two," the voice says with estranged finality. "And I am blind in this rejuvenation?"

"Mine is the only wick to have spontaneously combusted. I've had to mentally light the others, including yours, which is, at this moment, out. All but you and I have since returned to pooled wax. Shall I try mentally lighting another candle-in-the-line?"

"Why not just summon up an artificial flicker, for the moment, dear? At least I can get my bearings that way. I feel hopelessly lethargic."

"Summoning an artificial flicker isn't in my repertoire, yet, mistress," Uxana reminds. "I'm newly promoted, remember? There was no time to bring me up to full speed before we waxed for the last flood."

"Then, let me try," Zila says.

Moments pass. The darkness stays dark.

"Zila?" Uxana asks finally.

"I'm too weak," comes the soft reply. "I can't see. What is this place? What is this happening?"

Uxana shivers, and not just from the cold.

"A rejuvenation malfunction," Uxana reminds again. "You were about to initiate an artificial flicker?"

"Is that in my repertoire?" Zila asks.

"Most things are in your repertoire," Uxana offers. "You're a Sister of Primary Color—Blue."

"Do you, my dear, like I, feel an absence of emanated energy to summon?"

"I feel quantities never felt before. I fear we may even have overslept into another purging flood, long overdue."

"I don't sense the energy of which you speak. In fact, what little power I possess seems to be draining, even as I speak. Why is that, do you suppose?"

"Let me try another candle," Uxana insists.

She finds the pile, feel-sorting through the waxy columns to find the one that's least flaky, soft, and riddled with worm holes. The one she chooses in desperation is misshapen, as if it had sagged after removal from its mold.

She sets the imperfect candle on the flat surface of a rock and hopes for spontaneous combustion, but it doesn't happen. She finger-locates its wick in the dark, squeezing it three times between forefinger and thumb.

"Lalina pertuxus reonlin," she chants, providing the initiatory mantra from memory. Then, she sits back and concentrates. A mental lighting isn't easy for her despite the last few hours of intense practice.

"I thought you were going to summon an artificial flicker," Zila says, a note of whining complaint in her voice.

"I thought *you* were going to summon an artificial flicker," Uxana says, trying to keep the whining complaint from her voice.

"I've tried," Zila says. "It's not happening."

"Qantum-lu spelinx," Uxana continues with an alternative chant, wondering if she should start all over, wondering if Zila's interruption has interfered with the necessary wick-lighting incantation.

"I'm cold," Zila says.

"Flixim palenum plodnominium," Uxana says, and waits. She thinks she's failed and prepares for a repeat when the wick of the candle suddenly ignites.

"Yes!" Uxana self-congratulates, only to see in the next instant the full horror of what her conjured light reveals.

Zila—if what appears upon the rock can actually be called Zila—is a wildly deformed conglomeration of live flesh and contorted blue candle wax resembling neither candle nor Primary Color Sister of The Sisterhood.

"I feel different; I still can't see," the thing says, the dimpled hole in the macabre collage elastically concaving and convexing with each word.

Uxana, despite her efforts to maintain consciousness, feels her knees buckle and make painfully hard contact with the stone floor. For her, at least, darkness returns.

#20 BY THE DAWN'S EARLY LIGHT?

Uxana is brought back to consciousness by a physically violent jolt. Her first thought is that Zila, or what's left of her, has somehow managed to harness the power waves rippling through the air around them.

Zila, however, feels to Uxana possibly even more languid than before, and the girl in blue decides to make the best of a window of opportunity she doesn't know how long will exist.

"Zila, I need answers. Now!" Uxana insists.

"Focus! Focus!" Assuming Zila's eyes by all rights should be somewhere near her 'mouth,' it's impossible to determine where to look to engage and encourage Zila. Sniffling, Uxana continues stating the obvious: "I haven't a clue how to handle this, Zila, You have to help me. You must know something."

"For answers, you will need to consult the Book of Answers," Zila says.

Uxana wonders if her wax-and-flesh mentor is losing consciousness, submerging into sarcasm.

"Yes, certainly the Book of Answers is one way," Uxana agrees. "Not having it, though, you're going to have to make do."

"I'm beyond doing," says the blue-wax maw that undulates more than moves. "In fact, I'm nearly done."

"No!" Uxana insists.

The combination of flesh and wax quivers as if a magnified version of the flame wavering atop the lop-sided candle beside it. Upon the resulting wavy, mirage-like, reflecting surface, an image of the once-whole Zila appears, like a previously snapped photograph projected upon a rolling wave.

"You must be the one to focus, Uxana!" the visage insists, then fades, in the process solidifying into its previously monstrous form.

"Focus on what?"

"On what I need to mentally tell you, now," the waxy blue indention issues, only half-distinguishable as speech. Finished, it punctuates telepathically with a thought of Uxana hauling the mess on a plate of rock to the lip of the cave.

"Now?" Uxana half-thinks, half-asks aloud.

"With what little I have left, I sense something there that you need to see."

"Shouldn't I stay and monitor your candle?"

"The candle you have lit is now little more than a pool of dead wax, my dear. You know that; I know that."

Uxana is reluctant to touch the mass of flesh and wax that is all that's left of Zila. When she does, she's disturbed by the rapidly changing heat and cold, the soft and hard, of the contrasting admixture of reflective and dull.

Somehow, she manages to scoop up the wriggling mass to slip a flat rock underneath her one-time mentor. Reverently, Uxana carries what's left of her blue Sister to the vertical slit that connects the world inside to the greater world outside.

"You've brought us here to see the dawn together?" Uxana wonders aloud.

"What red dawn is it that rises in the West instead of the East?"

Uxana senses distraught, frantic human beings just beneath the pretty pink tinting the skyline of the Western horizon.

"One of but many monsters yet to come is already serving up a human barbecue," Zila says cryptically. "More and worse will occur if you don't find a way to intervene."

Without forewarning, the flesh and wax monstrosity half-crawls, half-flows over the edge of its stone base and slips down the precipice.

Uxana makes a grab, momentarily holding it.

"Don't be a fool, child," Zila pleads. "Not fallen, I'm but a hindrance."

Still, Uxana determines not to let go. Even so, powdery bits of what had been Zila embedded within blue candle wax are all that too-soon remain in her clutching fingers. Uxana reflexively, frantically, washes her hands in midair, releasing the remaining candle dust that floats slowly down to rejoin the majority of Zila, late great Primary Blue Candle of the Sisterhood, that moments before had made a sickeningly loud thud on the dry-as-bone canyon floor that was still echoing off the steep canyon walls.

#21 STRIP POKER, ANYONE?

"Ace of spades," Roman Michaels says.

Across the green, felt-covered table with its green, felt-covered divider, Jordan Tolms lifts the leading edge of a face-down playing card and takes a peek.

"Damnation!" he says. "Do you know that, during this go-round, you've only missed two out of the whole deck?"

"You're kidding!" Roman combs a hand through his silky hair. The disturbed strands catch the light behind him, providing a momentary halo.

"Come now, Roman! Fess up! You must feel it. You've never had a success rate like this one."

"Something about the air?" Roman hasn't made a statement. He's just not sure he's experiencing *anything* at all differently. "There's just, maybe, something different."

"Like what?"

"Like...well, you know...how it sometimes feels different before an electrical storm? Like that."

"Why don't I feel it?" Jordan wonders aloud.

"Maybe I'm just imagining it," Roman retorts as if he might actually have an answer.

Silently, Jordan wonders why and how Roman's perception seems on the sudden increase while Jordan's seems to be failing more and more lately. The last time Jordan read a deck of playing cards, he only got twelve right. At one time, he could consistently get thirty out of fifty-two.

"Let's try it once more," Jordan insists.

"Sure," Roman agrees after checking the time. His wristwatch is a very expensive but unassuming one that Gregory bought him when Roman read half the playing deck correctly. Gregory will be genuinely pleased by Roman's latest progress, especially if provided an equally impressive encore.

"Okay, then. Let's make it more interesting, shall we, by shuffling two decks?" Jordan says.

Roman frowns. Like when his brother, Sydney, smiles, Roman's dimples deepen; the corners of his eyes crinkle attractively. There's less likely to be another expensive gift from Gregory if Roman's skills, in reading a more challenging double deck, don't match the one-deck reading lead-in. "Shouldn't we first verify my one-deck success story isn't a fluke before we move on to something more complex?"

"A reading of all the cards but two in a regular

deck is spectacular success, Roman," Jordan says. "I mean, genuinely spectacular." He should know. He had doubters gawking in disbelief when he was able, in his prime, obviously now passed, to get a correct reading of just thirty. Not waiting for Roman's approval, Jordan reaches for a new deck, breaks the seal and peels off the cellophane wrapper. He opens the carton and spills the cards into one hand.

He reaches for the deck already in use but changes his mind, sliding it to one side, and unwraps a second new deck, adding its cards to the ones already in his hand.

He kid-shuffles them. He does a couple two-deck shuffles. Combining the two decks, he follows with a total of ten one-deck shuffles.

Dealing the top card, face down, onto the green felt on his side of the panel-divided table, he nods for Roman to begin.

"Ten of diamonds," Roman says, without hesitation.

Jordan thinks, "Four of spades."

He upturns the card.

Ten of diamonds.

He deals a second card, face down and nods for Roman to continue.

"King of Clubs," Roman says, again without

hesitation.

Jordan thinks, "Queen of Hearts."

He upturns the card.

King of Clubs.

So it goes, until fifty-two of the hundred-and-four cards have been placed, face down, one by one, on the table top. Mid-point score: Roman, fifty-two. Jordan, zero.

"He's hot," Roman says, wiping his slightly sweaty forehead.

"Who's hot?" Jordan reflexively asks. Unless Roman refers to the Jack of Diamonds, the last card upturned, his comment is entirely out of context. Jordan pauses, waiting to hear more from Roman.

"Timothy Gril's father," Roman says. There's a glassiness to his eyes, too.

"I thought it was your brother who was gay."

"I don't mean hot that way," Roman says. "I mean close-to-witch-burning hot."

"How can you possibly know that?" Jordan asks. He deals another card.

Without waiting for Jordan's nod, Roman says, "Six of clubs."

Jordan thinks, "Four of diamonds."

He upturns the card.

Six of clubs.

"Burn, heathen, burn!" Roman says disconcertingly loudly.

"Roman?" Jordan is suddenly concerned. "Are you all right?"

"Sure." Roman runs a hand through his hair and smiles. His dimples deepen. The corners of his eyes crease attractively. "Why do you ask?"

"You just said the most extraordinary thing about the father of someone called Timothy Gril."

"Did I?" Roman looks confused. "Don't really even know Timothy that well. He doesn't run with my crowd, if you know what I mean. As for his father, I've never met the man, although I think Gregory knows him quite well. How am I doing with the cards, this time around, by the way?"

Jordan decides not to pursue the Gril line of inquiry. Stranger things have happened during card-readings by major adepts, their minds working in entirely different ways from normal folk. Jordan can attest to that from personal experience.

He deals another card.

Again, without waiting for Jordan's nod, Roman this time says, "Two of clubs."

Jordan thinks, "Two of diamonds."

He upturns the card.

Two of clubs.

Out of sight and out of mind, Gyle Gril's flesh crisps, and he screams for deliverance at frustrated firemen who simply can't get close enough to try and rescue him due to the intensity of the flames.

#22 "P" MARKS THE SPOT

Images flicker by, in steady succession, one after another, in the roiling candle flame.

It's not the night moon in the sky which he finds so disturbing. It's that it isn't a full moon, already waning because of the light spilled by the dawn cresting the eastern horizon and painting wispy clouds the color of wet blood.

Up to now, his transformation to werewolf happened only when the moon was full. Regular as clockwork. No exceptions.

Up to now, his transformation from werewolf was complete before sunrise. Regular as clockwork. No exceptions.

Someone or something is gumming up the well-oiled mechanism! He suspected as much the minute the new kid on the block predicted a werewolf about to commence encounters of the third kind.

Natural order is, right this moment, being

interfered with. Could it be due to the acuteness of his lupine senses, that he detects change within the very air? Something destined to occur but about which no one, not even his fellow werewolves, knew, or knew and never bothered to tell him?

Whatever, he doesn't like it.

Nor does he like his increasing urge to clearly re-mark his territory. His task, begun in the early hours of the preceding evening, still isn't completed.

Who and what are these creatures, some of them unidentifiable to him, who are intruding and have the sheer audacity to mark as theirs what is his, and his alone? And where are they to be crisscrossing his terrain, yet remain undetected? It's as if he, alone of all, must defy convention and the rules of natural order, to dare be out in burgeoning daylight beneath a quickly fading moon.

He stops abruptly to sniff the air, confirming that the nearby scraggly bush reeks with a scent that isn't his.

Whose? What's?

Not the shape-shifter's, though he initially suspected such. The shape-shifter caused all sorts of mischief his last trip through. Piddling here. Piddling there. Piddling everywhere. It has been necessary to stop and drink twice just to produce the urine needed to mask the traces that the feline/serpent/wolf splattered across the landscape. Such a foul smell, too. This new stench, though, is even more pungent and putrid.

He nuzzles the thin and weak branches made brittle and lifeless more from lack of water than from the shape-shifter's golden shower.

He smells cat scent, but what cat? He smells snake, but what snake? He smells ... what else? Not wolf! As part wolf, he can recognize the scent of his own kind, even when combined with others. No, this is something else, altogether. He's smelled it before. But when? Where?

His memory finally serves him: It's a barnyard smell! Except, what shape-shifter would chose to become a placid cow? But it's not cow. Horse? It's not horse. An ass? Not an ass, or chicken, or goose, or duck.

It's a... surely not! Oh, but yes, it definitely is. It's the scent of a stinking, garbage-eating goat! Why, in the world, would any shape-shifter, ever, in sane mind...

Warnings deep inside him scream above his thoughts that his return to human form is about to begin.

He's conflicted. His need to completely mask the foul cat/snake/goat odor with his own, his need to continue a full exploration of his territory, to eradicate all traces of others, his need to be in his own bed when his conversion to human form occurs, all are fighting within him. Quickly passing time, though, puts him on the run to reach his home, his room, his bed, before he's missed.

He barely makes it, leaping through an open window, sliding beneath the covers.

The doorway to the hallway opens.

"Come on, buddy, rise and shine!" his father insists. "You don't want to miss early-morning wrestling practice."

#23 IN THE MOURNING

"Come on in, Timothy, and take a seat," Tom Mildon says.

Tom is fascinated by how people in general, teenagers in specific, handle stress and mourning. He's recently taken the job of psychologist at Flicker High School just for moments like this one...and like the one presenting earlier in the day with Trish Remoth. Of the two teens, Trish, the victim of a kidnapping, seems the more agitated. Timothy, although faced with his father's death, seems surprisingly nonplussed. Both seem prime candidates for inclusion in the book of case studies Tom is writing.

"How are you holding up, Timothy?" Tom asks in his very best grief-counselor voice. "You could take a few days off from school, you know."

"I have a report to give in geography," Timothy says, fidgeting in his seat, eyes focused on the floor between his feet. He adds, "Next period," as if afraid his session with Tom might run over.

"I know that your geography teacher..." Tom retrieves his reading glasses from his desk to scan the paperwork in front of him. "...Miss Revet, is it?..." Timothy nods. Tom removes his glasses and puts them back on the desk. "...would make every effort to work around you."

"I have the report ready now," Timothy states as reason enough for his being at school.

Fascinating! "And how is it working out at Mr. Ranlin's?" Tom asks. Strange...no, interesting...how it just so happens that Gregory Ranlin took over guardianship of the kid on the very evening of Timothy's father literally burning to cinders.

"It's okay." Actually, it's more than okay. The Ranlin house is enormous. Timothy's bedroom is bigger than the whole Gril family residence—before it burned down. Mr. Ranlin is a hands-off kind of guy, even if he is a vampire. Not only that, but Gregory's other two wards, Sydney and Roman Michaels, both at the top of the Flicker High A-list, don't seem to have found Timothy's addition to the household as any kind of imposition. Quite the contrary, they've been downright friendly. This bodes well. Timothy expects a forthcoming elevation of his status in the social hierarchy of Flicker High, after being stuck down near the bottom for what seems an interminably long time.

When the teen seems content to leave it at that, Tom gently prods, "Mr. Ranlin, I understand, was a long-time friend of your father?"

"Yep." Timothy stops there, although he has a whole story memorized. About how Gregory knew of Gyle Gril's long-time drinking problem. About Gyle's bad habit of burning candles. About how Gregory had long feared for Timothy's safety, not to mention the safety of Gyle. About how Timothy's father had finally been persuaded to let Timothy legally stay with Gregory, at least for awhile, and not a minute too soon. "I don't really want to talk about any of this right now," Timothy says.

Tom envisions their progress like pulling teeth and obliges by going statue-like behind his desk. He remains that way, unspeaking, unmoving, for the next half an hour. He doesn't even move when the bell rings to announce the beginning of the next period.

"I have that geography report to give, now, Mr. Mildon," Timothy says.

Only then does Tom respond. He shakes his head, disoriented, confused.

"The bell has already rung," Timothy reminds. "I'll need a hall pass."

Tom shakes his head, checks the clock on the wall, his wristwatch. He's unable to believe the time. The last thing he remembers...

"Mr. Mildon? You okay?"

Tom's not at all sure he's okay. He pulls out the front drawer of his desk for a blank hall pass and reaches for his glasses. His glasses are a twisted mass of lenses and tightly curled wire.

#24 GETTING TO KNOW YOU

It's the third consecutive time that morning in the gym that a pyramid of cheerleaders tumbles down into an awkward maze of ten teenage girls, accompanied by moans and groans. This time, Tania Quilnox provides a loud, "Ouch!" and rubs her right ankle.

All three collapses are attributed to Trish Remoth, not because the other girls are vindictive and spiteful—though they can certainly be that; not because the other girls are out to pass the buck—though each has certainly done that on more than one occasion. No, it's because all three times, plain and simple, Trish is the one responsible. Her balance, never off in the past, is off—way off—today. So far off, that she now believes her parents and sister were right to have suggested she stay away from school for a few extra days. So far off, that she now believes Mr. Mildon was right when he suggested she might benefit from just a bit more stay-at-home to recuperate.

Besides being concerned by her sudden lack of coordination, she feels further stressed by having to deal with the constant stares. She's well aware of the whispers, too, mainly rumors that she was drugged, then raped, then tossed, like a bag of garbage, up on the new kid's lawn.

Right now, she just wants things back to normal, whatever that is. Obviously, though, it isn't going to happen today.

"I'm going home!" she announces at last, picking up her backpack and heading through the door. A quiet, though easily detectable, sigh of relief sweeps through the room.

Unfortunately, the hall proctor, sitting behind his makeshift desk, jumps immediately on her case: "You have a hall pass, Trish?" he asks none-to-kindly when she almost collides with the desk positioned just outside the gym door.

Let the jerk give her a demerit. Let him report her. Who's going to be anything but sorry for the poor little girl who can't get herself together after having been abducted by someone or by something? Except...the proctor is none other than Johnny-Three-Spirits. What a coincidence. He's one of a group of her classmates who have avoided her like the plague since the incident. Wonder why? Or, rather, *not* wonder why!

She puts her hands on the desk's flat surface, right on the clipboard used for recording little (and big) violations of between-class rules. She leans forward, up close and personal. He smells, and not unpleasantly so, of pine trees in deep old-growth forests.

"We know it's you who did it," she says coldly, staring him in the eyes.

By "you" she doesn't specifically mean him. She is referring to Native Americans in general. Then again, by the sudden look of guilt that freezes on his face, maybe she does mean him—specifically Johnny-Three-Spirits. And what's with the "-Three-Spirits," anyway?

"It *is* you!" she dares guess. "Even now, I can see dog, cat, and snake whirling around inside of you. And when I tell my parents, and my sister, maybe even the police, that it was you, that it *is* you, what do you think they're going to do?"

He places the palms of both of his hands firmly onto the tops of her hands, then stands slightly using his full weight to pin her hands to the desk top.

"They'll think you're delusional," he says matter-of-factly. "They'll figure you're going crazy. They'll think you're batty, unhinged, suffering a nervous breakdown. A lot of people think that already."

"Maybe the police wouldn't believe me," Trish agrees, more certain than ever that, quite by chance, or maybe by freaky fate, she's stumbled upon the guilty-as-sin shape-shifter amongst them. "So, thank you for steering me away from their direction. Maybe a lot of ordinary people won't believe, either. But don't you think for even a second that my parents or my sister won't believe. And I think that once my sister hears about this, and about you, you're going to be up to your neck in barnyard crap. Because, even if I no longer have the power to slam you up against the wall and skewer you myself, like a bug on a pin, I assure you my sister can and will do it for me. You, being who you are —*what* you are—you must surely know that some powers are on the ebb, and others on the rise. Guess which end of that siphon my sister is on, you little creep."

"It was a mistake, you silly cow!" Johnny says,

lowering his voice and looking to make sure no one overheard. "We just wanted your sister to tell us what she knows about the blue girl."

"As if..." Trish provides a high, shrill laugh which she can't believe doesn't bring teachers and students on the run. She tries to dislodge her hands, but he has them really-really weighed down. "...that makes what you did any the less perverted and nasty!"

"We need to know about the blue girl. It's important, Trish. It's very important. It's more important than you, with your powers seeping away with each day, can possibly know."

"Then, you should have simply knocked on our door and asked my sister about the blue girl," Trish says venomously, imagining herself as Johnny, in snake form, spitting flecks of poisonous venom. "You shouldn't have kidnapped me—by mistake."

"True," he says with sudden humility. "It's still too early for us to know our friends or foes in the battle already being fought."

"Battle? What battle?"

"Ask your sister."

"Maybe I'll do just that as soon as you let go of my hands, you pervert!"

She's so surprised by how easily she slips free of him that she begins to fall over backwards. Johnny reaches for one of her flaying arms, takes hold, and steadies her, to keep it from happening. Her continuing lack of balance, especially needing Johnny to help her, makes her all the more furious. "Don't touch me, you weirdo!" she yells shaking her hand free. She turns on wobbly heel and heads huffily down the hall for the open outside door at the opposite end.

Unseen behind her, Johnny's three spirits manifest themselves, one after the other, before letting him return to his human form.

Johnny needs to let his grandfather know what's happened, but doesn't have a cell phone. Cell phones are banned at Flicker High as distractions from studies. Confused, frightened, calling on spirit, Johnny morphs into wolf. The floor beneath him goes slippery, his paw nails unable to get traction. He slides and slips, falling flat onto his belly twice, all four legs sprawling, before he successfully navigates out the doorway Trish just exited.

#25 DAM

As if an unwanted, unseen visitor breathes maliciously on it, the fire enveloping the glowing wick flickers, almost goes out, then sputters and bursts back into steady flame.

"The Grand Coulee portion of the Columbia River Plateau sets upon deep, underlying granite bedrock, formed forty to sixty million years ago," Sydney Michaels informs Miss Rita Revet's geography class.

Rita is finally able to concentrate on Sydney's class presentation. Just after Sydney began, Rita had been momentarily distracted, as had everyone else in the room, by Timothy Gril's late arrival. Pretty much everyone, including Rita, had assumed Timothy would be absent from all of his classes today and most probably the rest of the week, considering the terrible thing that had happened to his father. But that just went to prove that, whenever it involved students, to "assume" anything meant to make an "ass" out of "u" and "me."

"When the ice-age glaciers of the Pleistocene epoch appeared in the area," Sydney continues, "they scoured the Columbia River Plateau as far south as the highlands above Grand Coulee."

Rita enjoys hearing class reports, but less these days than in the past, when she didn't have to constantly monitor them so closely for plagiarism. Granted, students had always cheated, but computers made cheating so much easier, and, therefore, so much harder for teachers to recognize. Nowadays, she listened more for phraseology she'd heard or read somewhere on the web.

"Scientists used to think that glaciers diverted the Columbia River to create the truly unique geological features we have right here, around Flicker," Sydney says. "These days, though, they are tending more to believe that the formations resulted from massive glacial floods when water from Lake Missoula, in far-off western Montana, periodically broke its banks every several million years."

Rita now requires that every one of her students provide her with hard *and* digital copies of every report. She has, in her modern teacher armamentarium, access to several proprietary computer programs that allow her to submit anything questionable, and receive immediate feedback as to whether any portion of it appears, in any shape or form, on the internet. When she announced her acquisition of the programs to her classes, she hadn't been encouraged by the loud moans and groans that had occurred from each and every student.

"These glacial floods left behind channeled scablands, our very own Dry Falls area being one," Sydney ties things up by way of conclusion.

The rambunctious applause he receives has more to do with his popularity among his peers, with the exception of the teacher and Melissa Remoth, who are actually interested in anything geologic.

"Excellent!" Rita approves. Sydney is a genuinely adept student. Neither Rita nor any member of the faculty—as far as Rita knows—has ever found him cheating.

"Timothy," Rita says, "would you like to take up where Sydney has left off, or would you prefer we give you a couple more days?"

Timothy stands and prepares to speak; Rita wouldn't have been in the least surprised if he'd taken advantage of her offer. It is a rare student, this day and age, who doesn't take advantage of every opportunity to procrastinate.

Timothy assumes a position at the head of the class, in pretty much the same spot Sydney gladly vacates.

"Right here in central Washington State," Timothy begins, "is a three and a half mile crescent-shaped drop-off of land known as Dry Falls."

At that very moment, a short distance away, as the crow flies, from the very geological formation to which Timothy refers, girl-in-blue Uxana Uxl not-too-patiently tries to sort out the purple-colored wax from the myriad, damaged candles that had once held—but no longer do—the life-forces of her fellow Sisters in the Sisterhood.

#26 CHIMERA, CHIMERA, IN THE LIGHT

There's growing evidence of so much going wrong.

Other than, Zila's partial resurrection and subsequent suicide.

Other than all Sisters of The Sisterhood, except for Uxana, all dead.

There's also the undeniable heat of the day and the dryness of the air.

Before now, these last two omens of impending disaster had been ignored. Uxana has been spending so much of her time inside the cave's insulating embrace that she hadn't noticed them until now. In fact, she'd been, more often than not, cold. Now, forced to glean purple wax within the light at the lip of the protective cavern, she must confront the dire reality of the onerous heat and dryness.

What happened to the icy breath of the glaciers?

Where is the refreshing moisture that used to blow west from Lake Missoula?

How near is the next, long-overdue, watery purge?

Her mind wanders. Not good. She has too many important things she needs to do before the next flood happens.

For now, she must continue to fetch candles from the pile, and from them, salvage as much purple wax as she can. Only purple wax. Only old, purple wax. No way could she, these final days, harvest any other color wax and expect the resulting candle to meet the necessary criteria.

Surprising, how much information Zila—or what had once been Zila—had been able to impart within those so-very-few moments of telepathic contact. Surprising, how little of it provided any solution to the imminent threat growing in strength minute-by-minute before her. All Zila could manage to impart in those precious few moments was a possible means to that end. Newly-initiated Uxana would have preferred a more concrete blueprint for bringing on the flood. What if asking the purple candle the whereabouts to the Book of Answers didn't work? What if asking the Book of Answers the formula for bringing on the flood didn't work? What if she can't construct the required purple candle in time?

After all, there was surprisingly little useful purple wax to be found. Much of it had long-since crusted and become useless for candle-making. Some of it had been devoured by bugs, and disappeared, or become flecks of fossilized feces. Some had morphed into pieces too solid to be made malleable by basking upon hot rock in sunshine.

And what of the additional bad omen she hears in the distance?

Baroarhiss! Baroarhiss!

Some animal to which Uxana can't put a name. A sound heard sometime before in her distant past, if only she could just recall the where and the when.

She stops scraping the purple wax from the candle couched in her lap. Her right hand, holding the scrape-stone, is resting upon her knee.

She mentally replicates the sound of the unknown beast and sends the sound in search of its source which she knows lurks somewhere within her gone-stale, weary mind and memory.

Immediately, she's regretful. The old-wax purple candle must be made as soon as possible. Uxana's Sister, before suicide, made no allowance for visits from beasts in the light.

Uxana returns to her assigned task until the candle in her lap has no more purple wax to offer. She lays the deconstructed column of wax and the scrape-stone to one side. Carefully, she folds her blue robe about the precious wax to transport it to the stone that grows ever hotter in the increasing sunshine. The moment it touches the hot stone, the wax softens to touch. She takes a moment to mix the already melting mass, then mashes down the resulting lump, kneading it like dough, in order to allow the heat to permeate the invaluable whole.

Satisfied, at last, with her progress, she trudges back into the cavern, no longer fooled by its coolness, and scavenges the candle pile for three more candles. She wearily brings them back with her to the sunshine at the vertical opening of the cave.

Frustratingly, she realizes she has mistaken, in the darkness, a black candle for purple. She now only has two candles to mine before having to return for more.

She sits. She retrieves her scrape-stone and begins harvesting old, purple wax from the two just-fetched candles.

Baroarhiss! Baroarhiss!

She shudders in sudden recognition of the source of the sound. She remembers, now, she had not, in the past, heard it directly from the animal, but from a Sister who had learned to imitate it from another Sister who had learned to imitate it from another Sister who had supposedly heard it from the mouth of the beast.

"That is how a chimera sounds," Sister Zlu Xaxin had said, "from the time before the floods, when wicked magic was so strong that it could take physical form and live."

The magic, hereabouts, so long not purged by a

deluge that it, once again, reigned powerful enough to lure the part lion, part goat, part snake creature back to its old hunting grounds?

The horror of what she has asked, and moreover, what she is doing, grips her. While listening to the chimera's call, she has been unknowingly scraping away at the candle of Sister Mlin Tlalun. Mlin was a good friend. The two had roomed together for many years before Uxana had been formally initiated, just before last flood-time. Mlin, so young, and Uxana never to see her again. Never to see any Sisters ever again.

Suddenly, Uxana feels the weight of being totally alone. She is the last of her kind and feels responsible for correcting all that has somehow gone wrong, but she doesn't feel up to the task.

I wish I were one of the dead! she allows herself to think, the only one within hearing—except, maybe, for the malicious chimera nosing about somewhere in the scrublands nearby.

Helplessly, Uxana Uxl begins to sob.

#27 SHAKE, RATTLE, AND FLOW

"How many have seen Niagara Falls?" Timothy

asks, continuing his report. "Dry Falls, when it wasn't dry, was ten times bigger. In fact, it's thought to be pretty much the biggest waterfall that ever existed—at any time, anywhere. Lake Missoula flood water came barreling down through the Upper Grand Coulee and made the 400-foot drop over the rock face at sixty-five miles per hour, like a train gone amuck."

While Timothy always gives excellent reports, he's thought by his teacher, Rita Revet, to be exceptionally cogent in delivering this one. Rita continues to marvel at how the kid, his father burned to cinders just hours before, manages to keep it together. She thinks she just may ask Tom Mildon why some kids cope so well and others don't. It would give her a chance to engage Tom in a conversation, and Rita is sweet on the school psychologist. This would be a great way to get Tom to pay more attention to her.

"Twenty-thousand or so years ago, when ice-age glaciers plugged the Clark Fork of the Columbia River, all of the water in Montana suddenly had no place to go," Timothy continues. "What happened was that all of that excess liquid puddled until a large portion of western Montana was covered, in places, up to two-thousand feet deep, in one gigantic Lake Missoula."

Rita doesn't know why more of her students, some of whom are already fidgeting and whispering to one another, don't find this fascinating, considering it all happened in their collective backyard. She can tell just by looking, that few of them, with the exception of Melissa Remoth, the daughter of the *au pair* of geologists, give a damn. And since Timothy isn't yet officially anywhere near the top of the student body's A-list as regards popularity—although he might well soon be, having moved in with the very popular Michaels brothers—he isn't receiving much attention on purely social merit. For the moment at least, few of his peers care if Timothy gets teed off at them, or not, by their failing to pay attention to what he has to say.

"Periodic ruptures of this ice dam," Timothy says, "would drain the lake and cause flooding over most of Washington and northern Oregon. After each drain, the ice dam would re-form, and Lake Missoula would refill to the brim until the dam would break again. The end result was a succession of floods between fifteen-thousand and thirteen-thousand years ago. Some scientists estimate that there may have been as many as twenty-five floods in all."

It's at this point that Timothy is required by Miss Revet's guidelines to literally say, "The End." Miss Revet implemented this because she had been lulled so many times into thinking a student was done when he or she actually had more to say. Official announcement of the end saves everyone, especially her, the embarrassment of one of those oh-oh-sorry moments.

Timothy, though, who has in the past always willingly complied, doesn't do so this time. He has a "The End" in the works that will do the job far better and far more impressively, in his opinion, than he could ever manage with Miss Revet's expected stale sign-off.

On cue, Flicker High begins to tremble—a loud, low rumbling from somewhere distant. The air goes opaque with dust. The glass of one window cracks, with the sound of a gunshot.

"Earthquake!" someone yells.

Everyone dives for cover. Everyone that is, except for Timothy Gril and Melissa Remoth, who remain right where they are, locking calm, cool, and knowledgeable gazes across everyone else's frantic squeals and scrambles.

#28 ROLLIN', ROLLIN', ROLLIN'

Melissa catches up to Timothy during the mass exodus of students and faculty from the school building.

"Very impressive," she congratulates. "Think you can teach me how it's done?"

"Didn't do it," Timothy confesses. "Just felt it oncoming. Actually, I suspected you might have done it."

"Me? Get real. I read candles; I don't shift tectonic plates."

"I just thought the way you were so calm and cool about it . . ."

"Wasn't me, I promise."

"Then, I guess we're both lucky the roof didn't come down on our heads."

"Loved the way Miss Revet screamed bloody murder and almost ripped off your shirt trying to pull you down with her under her desk," Melissa says with a smirk.

Melissa spots Briana James, bloody paper towel in hand, pressed to bloody forehead, being ushered toward the oncoming ambulance sirens by Mr. Craine.

"Hey, Briana! Seen my sister?"

Briana looks at Melissa with a put-upon expression of someone with far better things to do. "She took off from cheerleading practice early," Briana finally says, as if she prefers being an earthquake victim to playing messenger. "Said she was heading home."

Mr. Craine insistently moves Briana along; Melissa and Timothy follow behind, at a slower pace.

"Sydney and Roman are convinced she's a witch,"

Timothy says.

"They're not alone. My sister referred to her as one just the other day," Melissa adds.

"Not 'bitch'. They're talking 'itch' with a 'w,' not a 'b'. Eye of newt, wing of bat. Bubble, bubble, toil and trouble..."

"You're serious?"

"That's what Sydney told me."

Now, there was a bit of information Melissa knew that her sister and parents would find very, very interesting.

"How is living with vampires, these days?" she veers the subject.

"Only one vamp, babe. The Michael brothers haven't yet gone over, or you wouldn't be seeing the two of them over there right now." Roman and Sydney form an isolated threesome with Cooper Loor.

"Is it true Sydney and the new kid are already an item?" Melissa asks.

"Certainly appears that way to me."

"You don't think Sydney is merely on a fishing expedition to see if the Loors know anything more about my sister turning up on their lawn than they've made public?"

"I'd say there's definitely more going on between Sidney and Cooper than just an exchange of information. By the way, how is your sister managing?"

"She decided to go home early, so probably not all that well," Melissa diagnoses. "She's never really been into this magic stuff and the increase of it, all around her, has really set her on edge, especially her abduction by that shape-shifter."

"Any closer to identifying who it is?"

"Not that I know, but we'll find out eventually, even if you and I, and my parents, have to do some serious group candle-readings."

Both of them break off conversation for a moment to reflexively sniff the air.

"Aftershock!" they announce loudly in two-part harmony.

Immediately, the ground rises beneath their feet and rolls eastward, re-conjuring screams and confusion in it's wake.

"Tell me you didn't do that just so you could hold my hand," Melissa says. She lifts her hand in question to prove that it is, indeed, firmly grasped within Timothy's.

"Funny, but I was just going to ask you the same thing," he says with a wide smile.

"You think there's something going on between us besides the exchange of information?"

"Could very well be," he says. "What do you

think?"

#29 TO BEE OR NOT TO BEE

For Jimmy-Who-Knows, nothing better illustrates the enduring Magic of the land than the long-lasting existence of the scrubland bee. The tiny insect, still officially unknown to science, has been helpmate to the shamans of Jimmy's tribe for as long as his people's oral history has been passed down from medicine man to medicine man.

Individually no bigger than the tip of Jimmy's little finger, and existing in totally nonaggressive swarms, they've most likely survived as long as they have by successfully avoiding people.

Though possessed of a stinger, it's only on very rare occasions, probably by accident, that one is ever used. More importantly, they can easily be persuaded, if politely asked using the correct chant, to share, usually without too much protest, any amount of honey or wax that they might have within their hives. Not that Jimmy or his forefathers would have ever taken advantage. Still, the honey and wax of the scrubland bee, a rich and luscious shade of gold, is as magical as the miracle-workers that produce it.

Neither Jimmy, nor anyone he knows, or has ever known, holds the secret of how the honey and wax are produced from what the bees have available in a landscape pretty much devoid of flora. Some might think that the expansion of the desert community of Flicker, replete with flower beds, provides a bountiful source of nectar and pollen. Some might think that, even before newly discovered water made Flicker's expansion possible, the landscaping of the U.S. Air Force base presents a veritable grocery store to the bees. Except, before Flicker, before the Air Force, the scrubland bees were producing their wondrously sweet and sticky, waxy-honeycomb-contained, dark golden ambrosia in more than sufficient quantity for millions of generations.

For Jimmy, nothing better proves his growing inability to tap the Magic of this place than his failure to summon even one scrubland bee, despite his having carefully used the correct summoning mantra. His only hope now is in simply locating a hive, before persuading Melissa Remoth to join him and his grandson, Johnny, in candle-making and candle-reading. To do this, he'll obviously have to call upon his grandson for assistance, despite the fact that Johnny's access to the Magic of the place has increased so fast and furiously that the boy still can't, yet, adequately control it.

Jimmy is made dizzy by another aftershock. He puts his hand to a boulder to steady himself and regain his sense of balance. Not that long ago, he would have sensed an earthquake well before its arrival, and would have known before each and every follow-up tremor rolled through.

Suddenly, he's aware of a scrubland-bee swarm, launched next to his hand by the latest ground tremor. He removes his hand, and the bees resettle.

The slit in the rock, their landing patch, is clearly not their hive. That they don't head off for it tells Jimmy, more than any magical intuition, that the earth is scheduled for additional rocking and rolling.

Quickly, he surveys the surrounding area, using what little is left of his fading magical powers to mentally search for the abandoned hive.

Just as he frustratingly resolves to accept that he'll need to wait and rely upon the bees to do the job for him, he spots their hive and is simultaneously tumbled to the ground by another uplifting of the ground beneath him.

He's down, trying to regain his footing, when the swarm begins alighting atop his head and torso.

Finding such actions uncharacteristic, he tells himself to be calm...these are, after all, his helpmates...even as they begin stinging him painfully.

#30 PICNIC TIME FOR TEDDY BEARS

It's Roger Remoth's day off. He and his wife sit mid-lawn, on a spread-out quilt, a one-time Christmas gift from Grandma Remoth, away from their house and its trees. They've a battery radio tuned to the local emergency frequency. The announcer is assuring them that there have been no earthquake fatalities even at evacuated Flicker High. Everyone is advised to stay put. The Remoths have their cell phones at hand, ready for incoming calls.

Bags of potato chips and other snacks, as well as bottled water, were scattered about.

And, oh, yes, they've invited Mr. Blumkins, the over-sized Teddy Bear that for years served as Trish's equivalent of a security blanket. Trish's mother, sixth-sensing Trish on the way, intuitively grabbed Mr. Blumkins just before exiting the house.

"Trish, thank God you're safe!" Mary says as soon as she sees her elder daughter approaching.

"You having a picnic?" Trish asks offhandedly, stopping near them and staring. How dare they look as if they're having a good time while the world literally trembles to pieces all around her?

"Everything was raining down inside the house," Mary Remoth says as if by way of explanation, "so we thought it safer to take up residence out here until the ground stops shaking. Mr. Blumkins was with us the last time around. Remember?"

"The earthquake that happened when you were six," Roger Remoth adds, seeing a look of quandary cloud Trish's face.

"I'm not six any longer," Trish reminds. Though she does still retain a lingering fondness and a genuine affection for her stuffed animal, she knows that Mr. Blumkins doesn't hold any solutions to her present problems. Trish only hopes, now that she has some partial answers, that her parents will be able to add to the growing vengeance-is-ours scenario.

"We heard they directed everyone to head home from your school," Roger says. "Some kind of structural damage to the buildings that they have to analyze, is it?" He leans to look behind his older daughter. "Where's your sister hiding?"

"Actually, I headed home before the earthquake, without Melissa," Trish admits, "as soon as I found out who our shape-shifter is."

Trish makes it sound as if her discovery was her reason for heading home early.

"Who is it?" Roger and Mary ask in unison.

"Johnny-Three-Spirits. And, before you ask, he admitted it, so there's no mistake. Just like Melissa suspected, he wanted to know what we knew about that vision of hers that included the girl in blue."

"Did we ever figure out how he could even know about that?" Roger wonders aloud.

The way Trish sees it, it doesn't matter how he knew. "Everyone seems to know, including that vampire, Gregory Ranlin, and his whole household. I think it's time we sit around one of your magical candles and conjure up a bit of discomfort for the pervert. No time like the present, either."

"Honey, neither your father nor I any longer have the power necessary to manage that," Mary apologizes. Not that she'd be quick to do it, on any account. "We tried again just this morning to see if we could pinpoint the culprit, and managed absolutely nothing, not even trance state."

"Best we wait for your sister, who's obviously better equipped," Roger suggests. "She might even have some suggestions."

"I don't want to wait around for Melissa or any of her suggestions," Trish says with sudden irritation. "If I have to do this cursing-by-candle business by myself, I can and will."

"Come on, babe," Roger argues. "You've never been all that interested in magic and never, to my knowledge, even attempted to develop any magical abilities. Whatever inherent skills you once had have gone as far south as mine and your mother's."

"You're both just getting old," Trish says, implying by the condescending tone of her voice that she is not. She wants support. She wants revenge. She wants restitution for having had her life screwed up royally by some weirdo Indian boy who can't seem to decide whether he's human, snake, cat, or dog. And she doesn't want to wait for her sister, who's probably off mooning over that pyromaniac now living with vampires. "I just need practice."

"Honey, you know that practice isn't the answer," Mary argues.

Trish, though, heads for the house. She's determined to get a candle, light it, read it, and send enough bad vibes Johnny-Three-Spirits' way to knock him on his Native American backside.

"Trish..." Roger and Mary call together after their daughter. Both desperately scramble to their feet. "...watch out!"

Whooooosh. Womp!

The pine tree, until just moments before one of several parenthesizing the Remoth house, falls so quickly, so nearly crushing Trish, that the startled girl is knocked over by the wind it generates in toppling.

#31 FRIENDSHIP, FRIENDSHIP, IT'S THE PERFECT BLENDSHIP

"Okay, Timothy," Sydney says as he runs over to join them, "if either you or your girlfriend plans on making the earth shake, how about letting me know beforehand? I mean, Timothy, you're family now— well, almost."

"We didn't do it," Timothy says. He doesn't argue the "girlfriend" part; neither does Melissa.

"Hmmmmm," Sydney stares, as if trying to decide whether to believe or not. He turns a head toward his brother and Cooper Loor, both watching nearby. "You two, over here!"

The summoned two saunter together on over and nod to Timothy and Melissa.

"You know my brother, here, right, Melissa?" Sydney asks. "I mean, who doesn't know my brother? And Cooper, here—I mean, your sister *did* turn up on his doorstep."

Actually, Melissa doesn't officially "run" with either of them. "Roman," she says in acknowledgement to Flicker High's tip-top-of-the-social-totem. To Cooper: "Thanks for bringing my sister in out of the cold."

"Right!" Sydney says. "Bro', beau', and a few mo' are heading on back, to play video games and lounge around the pool for the rest of the day. You want to bring Melissa along, Timothy, m' boy?"

"You want to come, Melissa?" Timothy asks.

"I'll have to check with my parents," Melissa says, stalling for time. She's not sure if she really wants to go into a vampire nest, or not. Then, again, it's pretty much only the school's A-list who ever gets invited, and Melissa is admittedly reluctant to turn down the opportunity now that it's been presented. Who knows when it will, if ever, be offered again?

"You can call them from the house," Sydney says.

"Did I mention I have to get home early tonight?" Cooper says. "My dad is making an effort to show up, and I feel obligated to be there."

"Well, as it happens, you didn't mention it, but I certainly wouldn't want to get in the way of any father-son bonding," Sydney says. "You want to check out early, I promise not to yell 'Party Pooper!' on your way out the door. Or, if I do yell it, just don't pay me any mind."

"Cooper, why didn't you tell us there was going to

be an earthquake? Aren't you a diviner?" Timothy asks.

"If you have a werewolf in your immediate future, Cooper will be the first to tell you about it," Sydney says. "Mere earthquakes, he can't be bothered with."

"Who has a werewolf in his or her immediate future?" Melissa decidedly wants to know. If it's true, that's something else her parents would definitely find of interest. Did they even know there was a werewolf in the vicinity?

"Your sister's boyfriend," Sydney says. His imitation wolf howls bring curious stares.

"Matty?"

"It was all very vague," Cooper emphasizes.

"Matty, a werewolf," Sydney says, making it sound eminent. "Tell your sister there'll soon to be another dog in her life." Quickly, he adds, "Hey, sorry." Everyone knows Trish Remoth's ravings about snakes, and cats, and dogs having lugged her through the wilderness area between Dry Wash Gulch and the Loor house, and Sydney realizes it wasn't the socially correct thing to push her sister's face in.

"Melissa?" Rita Revet interrupts loudly from a distance. "Your father is on the phone in Mr. Farling's office, and says it's urgent!"

#32 WHEN SHALL WE THREE MEET AGAIN?

Briana James, head bandaged from the cut incurred by a falling ceiling panel during the earthquake, lies on her bed, a large pile of pillows propped behind her against the headboard. In her lap is her mother's open Book of Spells.

Actually, Briana no longer considers the book her mother's, since Mrs. Silky James has lost the power to ward off even a common cold. That's her sneezing every few minutes in the background.

Georgiana Portland and Tania Quilnox, two of Briana's classmates, listen as Briana assures them that she, personally, found and cast the spell that is keeping all of them safe from catching her mother's sniffles. Had Silky had the presence to consult her daughter earlier, instead of making insistent attempts to cast the spell on her own, Briana could likely have kept her mom in good health, too. Some people just can't let go of their magic, even when it has exited stage right. Definitely uncool.

"So, are we going to do this, or not?" Briana asks, thinking she's found the spell that will do the trick the trio is currently after.

"I don't know," Tania vacillates. "You know what happened last time we tried spell-casting together: Your poor cat is still stuck to the closet wall. He's smelling badly by the way—or haven't you noticed?—and someone is bound to start nosing around soon."

"That spell was mis-indexed," Briana insists. "Instead of 'Simple,' it should have been listed under 'Moderately Complex.'"

"Well, how can we know how many others have been mis-indexed?" Tania wants to know. "Maybe we should ask your mother..."

"You think she, or either of your mothers, for that matter, is going to remember diddly-squat, ladies?" Briana says with an attending frown. "They've lost 'it,' or hasn't that dawned on you any more than it seems to have dawned on them? We three are all we have and need."

"Maybe Trish will just self-destruct on her own," Georgiana throws out for consideration. "In cheerleading today, even she knew she was really off on her timing."

"If you're willing to wait and take that chance..." Briana offers, shrugging. "Or, do you want to be sure she's taken out of the loop, so you can step in?"

"What about her sister?" Tania, ever cautious, insists.

"Little Melissa?" Briana asks, trying her best to sound not at all impressed.

"I heard she caused the earthquake."

"And if you believe that, I've a bridge to sell you in Brooklyn," Briana poohpoohs. "Let's get realistic, here. None of our mothers, even in their most witchy magical primes, could summon an earthquake like that, replete with aftershocks. So how in the heck could a mere candle-reader do it?"

"Still..." Tania is uncertain.

"You want to risk Trish 'accidently' tumbling another pyramid and really screwing up your ankle next time?" Briana argues. "You'd prefer Georgiana, here, having to fill in for *you*, instead of for Trish?"

"I'm just not sure how we'd explain Trish suddenly stuck to her closet wall," Georgiana inserts, her ankle still sore from her tumble earlier that morning.

"Oh, ye, of little faith!" Briana condemns, reasoning if Melissa per chance really is responsible for the earthquake—Briana rubs her bandaged wounded forehead—that's another good reason for giving the whole Remoth family a lesson by zapping Trish out of the prestigious cheerleading picture. "All we need do is chant together the 'Simple Spell of a Sore Neck,' and our little problem will be solved with Trish just being incapacitated enough so that the squad can get rid of her." She pats the bed on either side of her, by way of

117

inviting them out of their chairs to join her.

Ten minutes later, the girls have completed their spell-casting. At the Remoth house, Trish suddenly collapses to the floor, hands to her neck, eyes wide in disbelief, her neck muscles grotesquely swollen, twisted, and misshapen.

Trish's dad drops to his knees and tries unsuccessfully to identify his elder daughter's problem. Frantically, he calls for Mary to dial 911.

Before his wife can even pick up the phone, there's a loud gunshot-like crack, and her husband, grief-stricken, moans, "My God, Mary, I think Trish is dead!"

#33 ON BECOMING

The candle flame flares incandescently, and within its heart...

Johnny-Three-Spirits, as wolf, stops and sniffs the air. He tries to concentrate. He's being constantly distracted by strange smells that mask the one smell— that of his grandfather—that he wants to isolate.

What is that interfering half-man, half-wolf aroma? A werewolf?

What is that butt-in stench of cat, and snake,

and...goat? Another shape-shifter?

There are even hints of vampire, witch, warlock, diviner, candle-reader and smashed candle wax in the strange, electrically-charged heaviness of the air.

Added to that, the dust produced from the earthquake, aftershocks and accompanying falling rock has created a suspension of fine particles that constantly clog his nostrils, messing up his ability to follow the spoor of his grandfather in the scrubland. Rocks, shifted from where they were to where they are now, seem to intentionally block his pathway.

It's important that he tell his grandfather about his confrontation with Trish in the school hallway. It's important his grandfather knows that Johnny's shape-shifter abilities have once again slipped out of control. Morphs are occurring in the open, in Flicker High— Johnny, as wolf, had had to scramble on a slippery floor, like a spastic dog, to make his exit before anyone saw him.

Before him, loose rocks form a pile, tall, unstable, still emanating earthy ash, further impeding wolf's progress. Does wolf go over the top—too dangerous? Does wolf go around—not timely? Does wolf return home and wait for his grandfather to return in his own time? The latter isn't an alternative, if just because there's another scent Johnny has captured from the air.

It's the smell of his grandfather's fear. Possibly, the old man has fallen, as a result of the earth-shift. Possibly, he's injured. Possibly, he's dying, pinned underneath a rolled stone. The scrubland is a dangerous place under normal conditions even for someone as attuned to the ways of nature as a Native American. Unexpected earth tremors and toppling stone add yet more booby-traps, making it singularly perilous.

Johnny-wolf hunkers down on all fours. His muzzle slides across the ground examining a dark space between two particularly large base stones. Is there a glint of light somewhere in the distance? If so, it's a gauntlet too small for wolf. Wolf's heavy, well-muscled, furry body would too easily disturb the precarious stack from the inside-out, and likely see him squashed beneath it.

He shape-shifts to snake and slithers into the breach, tongue flicking repeatedly in an attempt to detect any odor-taste of his grandfather, or the faintest glimmer of sun-warmth from beyond the narrow obstacle course. His gliding body brushes against a side, and the pyramid of loose stones crackles and crunches, then sighs and moans above and on both sides of him. Even snake may be too large a thread to slip, successfully, through the eye of this particular needle.

Snake slows, trying not to hurry so recklessly. He

flicks his tongue several more times forward. A new heat source, other than sunshine, becomes evident just beyond the exit, encouraging him on. His head, exiting the hole, senses this second source of heat, unmoving, as human.

Safely out of the hole, snake morphs into Johnny.

For a moment, he's uncertain what he sees. It's obviously a human positioned in an unseemly sprawl upon dusty, gravel-littered ground. Obviously bloated, the face is so ballooned as to have bulbously folded its expanded flesh over eyes and nose and mouth, leaving mere pinpricks.

"Grandfather?" Johnny ventures.

It's not his grandfather, Jimmy-Who-Knows, who answers, but a loud, surrounding, buzzing sound.

A swarm of scrubland bees shrouds Johnny before he realizes they're even there.

#34 A SALINE SOLUTION?

Johnny's first defensive thought is to morph into wolf. If nothing else, dense fur will make it harder for scrubland-bee stingers to penetrate well-insulated flesh. The buzzing cloud, however, abruptly lifts, rising as quickly as it arrives into the air. Johnny watches the swarm as it constantly shifts its shape in formation and flies the short distance back to, and then disappears into, the rock-lined cleft serving as a temporary hive.

Reprieved, Johnny returns his attention to the bee-stung victim. If the bees, in acknowledging Johnny's presence, have returned to their friendly, passive, helpmate insect selves, then the young shape-shifter can attend to his grandfather without worrying further about the bees.

He isn't certain the venom-swollen man is even his grandfather; it seems to him very unlikely that two men would own the exact same gray flannel shirt, buckskin pants, and scuffed Tony Lama cowboy boots. Yet, whoever it is definitely needs help, although there's the good chance he's already well beyond help, Johnny's or anyone else's.

"Granddad?" Johnny asks, calling up his rescue options in his head.

One, he can morph into wolf or cougar and attempt the same kind of transport he'd managed with the unconscious Trish over the scrublands between here and Flicker. Certainly, Trish hadn't overly suffered—physically—in consequence, but she hadn't been bloated in shock from a huge overdose of bee venom, either.

Two, he can sit tight, do nothing, and hope the

victim's natural immune system will check in, full force, and begin the healing process, but there's no immediate indication whatsoever that the grossly swollen man is headed anywhere but farther down the road to oblivion.

Three, Johnny can...

Does he even have a third alternative?

He tries to focus. There is something from his past that he feels certain may help him in this situation, if he could only remember what it is. Concentrating on anything, lately, has proven to be hard as blazes. His grandfather explained it away as a shift in the area's power sources. Johnny doesn't have a clue if his grandfather is right or wrong; he just wishes that if the power sources in the area are shifting, they'd quit shifting for one little moment so he could think clearly.

Surprised when they seemingly oblige, he summons from his memories his incident with Qala, the Scorpion. A small scorpion whose sting, though not deadly, is painful in the extreme, as Johnny can bear witness, having been a recipient. Out in the middle of nowhere, with only his grandfather in attendance, Johnny bravely resolved to endure a prolonged period of painful discomfort until...what had his grandfather done?

Jimmy-Who-Knows had peed on his grandson's

wound.

The pain had immediately disappeared. The expected follow-up pain never happened.

Granted, one sting from Qala, the Scorpion, isn't the same as hundreds of simultaneous bee stings, but...

Johnny unfastens his grandfather's canteen from the man's belt and empties it of water. Standing and turning himself with the empty container before him toward the nearby rocks, he partially refills it.

#35 KISS AND TELL

Cooper's lips are firm yet pliant. They taste of peppermint.

Sydney so enjoys kissing them that he leaves his mouth in contact with them for far longer than he can remember doing with anyone else. Telling him what?

"Did you divine this was going to happen?" Sydney asks, having finally, reluctantly, broken the smooch. He recycles the savory, residual peppermint flavor on his lips by licking them.

"Well, I definitely did know this was going to happen," Cooper admits, "and it had nothing to do with divining."

His appetite whetted, Sydney shushes Cooper, and

reconnects lips-to-lips.

"Oops!" Roman says from the open doorway, deck of cards in hand. "Am I disturbing something?" He knows he is; his Cheshire-cat grin says as much.

"As a matter of fact, you are," Sydney confirms, reluctantly disengaging from Cooper. "Do me a big favor and get lost."

Cooper is neither embarrassed nor concerned by the interruption. He knows that Roman knows that Cooper and Sydney have had a man-o'-man-o' "thing" for each other from the get-go. Sydney, on the other hand, is more interested in further exploration of Cooper's lips than in anything his brother has to say. That is, until his brother says it.

"I just thought you might be interested to know that Trish Remoth is dead."

"What do you mean, Trish is dead?" Sydney hopes he misheard. "That why her old man summoned Melissa from the school?"

"I don't think so," Roman says. If he sounds uncertain, he is uncertain. He's still trying to sort through the sometimes cluttered flashings that remain fluttering in his mind after a session with the cards. "That come-on-home-Melissa, I think, had something to do with a tree falling and almost but not actually killing her sister."

"A tree?"

"Pine."

"You got this from the cards, or from the news?"

"Don't think it's on the news, yet," Roman says. "I'm not even sure the authorities know, or I suspect we'd hear..." He pauses, letting distant sirens provide punctuation.

"So, did she die because of the venom administered by the shape-shifter who grabbed her?"

"No venom according to the authorities, or according to Melissa, either, remember? And while the cops have been known to leak disinformation, Timothy seems to think Melissa is a girlfriend of her word."

"So, what do your cards say?"

"Actually, they hint at witchery."

"Witchery?" Cooper jumps in with genuine fascination. "For sure, we have witches in the area?"

"For sure, we have witches, and warlocks, and shape-changers, maybe even that werewolf you mentioned," Sydney says. "You already know there are a vampire, a card-reader, and several candle-readers. Flicker is becoming a regular convention center for beasties and weirdies."

"I'm wondering if you might like to read a candle to provide specifics, brother dear?" Roman suggests.

"Me? We might better enlist Melissa, after she

calms down from this latest bad news about her sister. You do remember that the candle-readers of our family, including me, have never been all that good in conjuring things in other than mish-mash, hazy, blacks-and-whites?"

"I've been meaning to ask you about that. If that's the case, how did you happen to know the mystery girl of your last reading was dressed in blue and toting a blue candle?"

"Well...you know..." Sydney stops, feeling uncomfortable. No doubt about it, he definitely told Roman and Gregory the mystery girl and the candle both wore blue. That was way before Melissa confirmed the color of the girl and the candle from her sister's reading. Had there, then, been an aura of blue in Sydney's vision that had been so contained within the overall usual murky dish-water blur that it escaped notice except by his subconscious?

"We all sense fluctuations in the rapidly escalating power grid of this place," Roman reminds. "Do you think while Gregory's powers ebb, yours, like those of Timothy, will increase in like measure, soon to include full, vivid color?"

"I don't know what to think." Genuinely, Sydney is at a loss.

"Will just an ordinary candle do?" Roman asks

and steps back to retrieve a fat blue one being used as a divider of books on the shelf above the turned-off television. "Or, need we scavenge one more specific?"

Roman lights the candle with a lighter he pulls from his pants pocket.

Sydney is immediately shock-waved by what's instantly conjured in the flame.

"Whoooaaahhhhh!" His response is defensively reflexive, the accompanying exhale so strong as to extinguish the flame and the vision.

"Come on, now, brother dear," Roman chides; Sydney has literally recoiled to the extent of lifting his legs up on the couch and arm-wrapping his knees. "Surely, even to a gay boy like you, our local witch, Briana James, can't be all that repulsive."

"That sure as hell wasn't Briana James," Sydney argues, "unless she's more grotesque and bloated than the Pillsbury Dough Boy. Not to mention having changed sex and being nearly dead somewhere in the middle of the scrublands."

For the moment, at least, neither the surprised Roman nor equally surprised Cooper asks if what Sydney saw was in living color—which it definitely was.

#36 THE PINE DIDN'T DO IT

Melissa and Timothy are three blocks away when the ambulance and the fire truck, close on its tail, sirens blasting, pass them by. The teenagers feel the warm wind, smelling slightly of oil and gas, which the vehicles leave in their wake.

"They're turning into my place!" Melissa forgets all about the pleasure of Timothy's company in his having offered to walk her home and starts running. Timothy follows, keeping up beside her.

The first thing Melissa notices that's different, besides the ambulance and truck out front, is the lone pine tree down in the front yard.

She's confused, though, because her father, on the phone, had specifically said the earthquake-toppled tree had missed Trish, and that Trish was all right. He'd said they wanted Melissa home for a family candle-reading. Apparently Trish identified the shape-shifter who abducted her, although Roger Remoth didn't want to discuss it further on the phone.

Roger waits for his younger daughter and Timothy at the front door. Two medics slip by to return to the ambulance for a gurney.

"Why don't you and Timothy wait out here, honey?" Roger suggests. He's not really sure what's appropriate under the circumstances.

"Is Trish okay?"

"Apparently the falling tree did do some damage, after all," Roger says, wrapping an arm around his younger daughter, now his only living daughter, and shifting her to one side of the porch, Timothy shadowing. "It just didn't become apparent until later."

"So, where is she?"

"In the house with your mother."

"She's going to be all right?"

"I'm afraid not, sweetie."

Melissa wants to scream but can't. She wants to cry but no tears come. Melissa wants to accuse her father of lying, given he'd minutes ago said Trish was fine, but the words don't come. Simultaneously, she's glad and mad that Timothy's presence somehow keeps her from expressing all of the pent up emotions seeking to erupt from inside her.

"I want to see her," she says, calmly, at last.

"Are you sure?" Roger asks. Had he been given the choice of seeing or not seeing his older daughter dead, he's not sure what he would have decided.

"I want to see her," Melissa repeats.

"Shall I wait out here?" Timothy asks. He's no surer of protocol, in such a situation, than anyone else seems to be. But since he's neither invited in, nor told to stay outside, he opts for the latter.

Melissa and her father go in.

Trish looks peacefully at rest on the couch where Roger has placed her. Mary Remoth is on her knees beside her older daughter, sobbing uncontrollably.

"Maybe she's just asleep," Melissa insists. "You know, in a trance or something," but even as she suggests, she knows it isn't so.

"I'm afraid not, honey," Roger says, tears welling in his eyes; Mary sobs louder.

"But how can she be dead?" Melissa wants to know.

Roger doesn't have a clue, except to think that adrenalin kept Trish from recognizing the resulting extensive internal head damage that must have been done. Roger feels guilty in not having called 911, right then and there, or taking her to Emergency whether she liked it or not.

Melissa, shocked, leaves her dead sister, her mother, her father, and walks aimlessly back outside.

She's initially comforted by Timothy being there to take her in his arms. A moment later, however, she's discomforted by her need to rant and rave and by Timothy being there to keep her, somehow, from doing it.

"She's really dead," she speaks into his shoulder.

"It didn't do it," he whispers into her ear, his breath hot and damp.

"It?" Melissa pulls away slightly. "Didn't do what?"

"The tree," Timothy says. "It didn't kill your sister."

"And how can you possibly know that?" Melissa, disconcerted, asks.

"Because it just swore to me it didn't do it."

#37 THE ROAD PAVED WITH GOOD INTENTIONS

"Hey, good buddy!" Madison Loo says as Cooper opens the front door and steps into the living-room.

"Dad!" Cooper responds enthusiastically.

The two meet to exchange brief, though firm and genuinely sincere, hugs.

One thing Cooper loves about his father is Madison's ability to show affection. Too many military brats have parents who act as if their kids are inmates in a military prison camp.

Another thing Cooper loves about his father is long-running good intentions. There are no doubts in Cooper's mind that his father sincerely wants to spend more time with his family, and would, if his job only let him.

"Been home long?" Cooper asks. If he'd expected his father to check in quite this early from the base, he would have left Mr. Ranlin's house earlier, even though Cooper was having a good time. Roman and Sydney Michaels continue to not only provide Cooper access to the top social rung of Flicker High, but Sydney is just the boyfriend Cooper has always wanted. He's attractive, smart, funny, and kisses like no one Cooper has ever kissed before, boy or girl. Not to mention that the brothers never fail to astonish with their revelations. Although Cooper has yet to hear it officially, he'd bet his money that Trish Remoth was dropped dead by the witchery of Briana James and a couple of Briana's spooky friends. Her death is going to be particularly hard on Trish's sister and, by default, hard on Timothy Gril who, now living with the Michaels brothers, is obviously sweet on Melissa. Poor Timothy, his father so recently up in flames, is getting dumped on royally lately.

"I've only been home long enough to convince your mother she can start cooking that promised crown roast. And, oh yes, to get into something comfortable." That he's wearing pajamas, his favorite old robe and felt slippers says more than anything else that he plans to settle in for the duration. "I do believe that's what she's doing right now. Sure you don't want to spend more time at your new friend's house?" His father is keenly aware of how difficult it is for military kids to have to constantly be making new friends.

The way he says "friend" contains no hint of "gay friend." Madison probably doesn't know that Sydney is gay, and Cooper sees no reason to tell him.

"I can see him any day. How often does my dad make it home to spend a whole evening with the family?"

"More often, these days, I certainly hope," Madison says, thoroughly convinced it's going to happen, his express reason for taking this assignment being to spend more time with his wife and son. "By the way, I just happened to stop off at the video store on my way here, and guess what I happened to find there?"

"Mmmmmm. 'All Quiet on the Western Front'?"

Madison loves war movies, any and all; even the B-ones, "All Quiet on the Western Front," a particular favorite.

"And for later?" he challenges his son to guess.

Madison has so many other favorites that guessing which one is next to impossible. " 'K-19: The Widowmaker'," Madison says, ending the suspense.

Madison is a dedicated Harrison Ford follower, possibly because so many people have told him that he looks like the actor who is forever stereotyped as the intrepid Indiana Jones, running around with dusty, bent-brim hat and trusty bullwhip; it's an image Madison finds particularly appealing.

Father and son drop down on the couch. On cue, Mrs. Loo brings in a big bowl of buttered popcorn, sets it mid-center on the coffee table in front of them, and returns to the kitchen. Her husband uses the remote control to trigger the DVD that's already loaded and ready for playing.

Madison and Cooper settle in, both content.

If Cooper intuitively knows that this will be the last time, in a very long time, that his father will make it home, he's not going to spoil the moment by telling. Madison will find out soon enough that a public-relations nightmare is about to erupt that'll have him and the Air Force scrambling, late into many a night, to try to keep it under top secret wraps.

#38 SO, WHY DON'T YA TAKE A PICTURE?

The candle flame pauses, momentarily, then resumes flickering, subtly changing in color from red to red-orange, as if transitioning, albeit smoothly, almost imperceptibly, from one reading to another.

Peter McGee loves the scrubland for taking pictures. There's something about its weird rock formations—huge boulders rolled from hundreds of miles away by flood waters and left free-standing on stark slabs of cooled basaltic lava flow. The place presents all kinds of opportunities for artistic interpretation by a skilled cameraman.

His agent likes the pictures, too. As does the owner of the Whilman Gallery in Seattle. Phil Whilman likes them so well, he wants to include another couple walls of them in the exhibit of Peter's work announced for next Sunday.

What Peter doesn't like is being in the scrublands at this time of early evening. The place fills so quickly with darkness and shadows that it's downright creepy. That Peter is even here is only because it's the only time of day he's not yet photographed. To his thinking, if there was a boogieman, it would live here and emerge just after sundown.

The timer on his camera, set to capture what little remains of daylight on the surface of a rock formation, clicks, signaling the finish of the shooting. Peter immediately begins packing his gear. He wants to get back to his car as quickly as possible. He still has to sort the shots he's taken. Then, he has to get his agent and Phil Whilman's input on which ones to select.

Then, there's matting and framing and hanging to be done. Not to mention how this place continues to give him the willies.

He decides to take a short-cut to his car; one he's taken once before and sworn never to take again. It takes him along the outer perimeter of Rockpoint Air Force Base. He can still remember the brouhaha from last time. He'd spotted a genuinely interesting rock formation just across the fence and had stopped to snap a picture of it. Big mistake, the fence being monitored by surveillance cameras 24/7, and any photographing of the base strictly prohibited. The military police were over Peter as quickly as a swarm of bees. His film was confiscated and never returned—a whole day of shooting down the crapper.

This time, he has no intentions of taking pictures of the Air Force's precious rocks. His camera equipment is securely hidden within his backpack; anyone watching will just see a hiker; though, now that he thinks of it, anyone crazy enough to be out hiking in the scrublands at this time of day-into-night would probably be suspect just on that account.

Still, Peter has things to do and people to see. Time is of the essence, and this place is getting more eerie by the second.

He reaches the fence and turns to walk alongside

it.

He tells himself that he isn't hearing sounds coming from within the rock formations behind him.

He tells himself that the heavy breathing he hears is his own.

He tells himself that he's a grown man and it's silly to think that there are beasts and beasties in this God-forsaken land, following and waiting around every bend to get him.

He keeps up a steady pace. He'd like to walk faster. He'd like to run. Yet, he doesn't want to look suspicious. Worse, he could trip in the dark and loose the camera, or even break a leg.

He keeps going, making certain he doesn't glance, even once, no matter how briefly, across the fence into military territory, lest someone come running. He can't afford to lose the precious shots he's captured for inclusion in his upcoming exhibit.

The force that hits him from behind knocks Peter hard to the ground. The weight on top of him keeps him pinned. The sudden stench of hot breath on the back of his neck makes him nauseous. The clamp of something sharp and powerful over, on, and around his head sends jagged pains skyrocketing through his brain.

Peter McGee is dead even before he knows he's dying.

#39 WHAT NUMBER ARE YOU CALLING?

Someone is actually calling Gregory. It's so unexpected, it's almost overlooked. It's so faint, it's almost unnoticed. After much effort expended in pinpointing its origin, the vampire decides it could very well be a bogus call or even a trap. Therefore, he purposely ignores it. Then, he changes his mind and veers back in the direction he's just sluggishly flown.

Having lost Gyle Gril as a blood source, Gregory is forced once again on the prowl. He has, for quite awhile, maintained a group of people he visits regularly to feed on, and he doesn't like to lose any of them. Losing Gyle was necessary, but that doesn't make the loss any less real, or any less an inconvenience.

Having had seven people available, one for each night of the week, he could, by night eight, return to dine on the first person on his list. Seven nights allow for sufficient replenishment of blood loss. While an adequate blood replacement might well occur in six nights or even less, Gregory doesn't want to take any chances, or break from his previously established routine.

So, here he is: Troubled. Irritable. Not feeling his best. In fact, feeling downright crappy, as he has for several months. Trying to round out to the magical seven the desired number of contributors to his well-being, hoping that in doing so, he won't leave any clues that might alert someone that there's a blood-sucking vampire loose in Flicker. With his vampiric powers on the ebb and his present state of lethargy, he doesn't need the added complication of vampire-killing crowds searching for him. To his advantage, the discovery of water near Flicker and the recent boom of real estate development in the area provides him with a population pool far larger than before from which to make his selection, with even less chance of being noticed.

He confirms the house emitting the extrasensory signal and chooses to gather his wits at the outside the downstairs window through which the call is loudest. Even now, close up, the call isn't as audible as such calls received when Gregory was in his prime.

He pauses. Considering the mischief originating from this particular house so recently, Gregory feels he has every right to be wary. Granted, the call seems to be coming from the warlock and not from the warlock's witchy daughter. That said, Briana James might well be attempting to exercise her increased powers to cajole her father's cooperation. To what end, though? Purposely killing an aging candle-reader is one thing; getting rid of a vampire is quite another, the latter being far more complicated and dangerous for both parties.

The long, sharp nail of Gregory's index finger scratches the window pane.

"Come in."

The window slides open, and Gregory flows inside.

Nalbot James sits in an easy chair next to and facing the window. "About time," he complains. "I've been calling you for days."

"To what end?" Gregory sees no one else in the room. But the Remoth girl was killed long-distance.

"To make me a vampire, what else?"

"A warlock wanting to become a vampire?" Gregory finds that somehow hard to believe, though even a marginally intelligent warlock would know the vampire is the superior being.

"My warlock powers have almost completely faded," Nalbot complains. "With my daughter's powers on the rise, she's becoming more and more impossible."

"Like her killing the Remoth girl, you mean?"

"She killed Melissa Remoth?"

"She killed Trish Remoth."

"Not quite as bad, still...I need an alternative power-base if I'm to deal with her and survive the coming times."

Nalbot tips back his head, placing his neck in high-relief. The skin of his throat stretches across his throbbing jugular vein like membrane atop a beaten drum head. Voila! Gregory's food source, number seven; his for the taking, no muss, no fuss, no bother. Except, strangely, uncharacteristically, Gregory isn't in the least bit hungry.

He does an about-face and leans out the open window, expecting to be airborne, but instead falls onto the ground outside with an unbecoming thud.

He's stunned. His injured ego isn't helped by the laughter behind him.

"It would seem, old boy, that you're in even worse shape than I am," Nalbot says, peering down at him from inside the house.

Gregory gets up, dusts off, straightens his shoulders and walks off down the street, Nalbot's laughter still painfully ringing in his ears.

"Thank the lucky stars," he mumbles to himself, "I didn't launch thorough a second-story window."

#40 WHILE I PONDER, WEAK AND WEARY

The chimera is definitely out there. So is the vampire. The werewolf. The shape-shifter. Other creatures, too, gathering in and around Flicker in increasing numbers. Most of them, Uxana wouldn't

want to meet after nightfall. Most of them, Uxana
wouldn't want to meet in the full light of day. Most of
them, she doesn't want to meet, period.

Lest they detect her presence, even see her at the
lip of the cave, she once again retreats into the cavern's
interior. There, she lights three dead Sisters' candles to
provide her with enough light to hold back some of the
increasingly cold darkness and make her feel less
afraid.

She doesn't light the purple candle. She hopes for
some sleep first, knowing full well that the faster she
finds the Book of Answers, the quicker she'll have
solutions to the growing problem of Flicker and the
creatures gathering there. On the other hand, she
doesn't want to attempt Magic when she's as exhausted
as she is. Making the purple candle has been tiring as
well as time-consuming. She's not even sure she's made
it right. She would have preferred a roaring fire, a pot, a
mold, a ladle, her Sisters about her, supporting her,
chanting with her. Instead, she had to deal with
shavings of wax, a barely warm stone, kneading not
melting, and a final less-than-esthetically pleasing wrap
of wax around a wick salvaged from one of the dead
Sisters.

Her purple creation looks less an instrument for
summoning answers than it does one for the sticking of

pins and the casting of evil spells.

She's afraid she's got it wrong. She's afraid that, when she lights it, the wick won't stay lit. She's afraid the wax isn't wrapped sufficiently. She's afraid she's tainted the purple with segments of colors of other dead Sisters prohibited from the mix. She's afraid she's wasted her time and effort.

Most of all, she's afraid that the purple candle will just burn to nothing, achieve nothing, leaving Uxana all alone, with only her haunted thoughts and dark creatures roaming the night outside her doorway.

She pulls her blue cloak more firmly around her to temporarily lessen the bone-chill, the candlelight about her providing respite from the darkness but little warmth. The coldness attempting to grip her is one of pure despair.

She still finds it difficult to get her mind wrapped around the reality that she's the last of her kind. Although it's hardly her Sisters fault for the circumstances that killed them, she blames them for not being here. She blames Zila for having resurrected as grotesque flesh and wax, ultimately suiciding over the escarpment.

She shuts her eyes. She hears a chimera roar and hiss, a werewolf howl, a shape-shifter's growl. She waits for the sound of the leathery flap of vampire wings, surprised when they don't join.

Earlier, she thought she even heard two human screams, an accompanying buzz dulling the first, an accompanying crunch accenting the other. Dragging sounds. Chewing sounds. Moans of pain and despair.

She shivers and tries to sleep, but she can't.

#41 IS SEEING REALLY BELIEVING?

Johnny stands guard as wolf.

Something about the onset of dusk, and now nightfall, has his nerves on edge. He intuits that he and his grandfather need more protection than he can provide in human form.

Maybe it's the undefined sounds of the night that forewarn of dangers unseen. Even the moon-howl of a brother wolf seems tainted and not quite right.

And what was that seemingly human scream? Why does the nearby buzzing of the scrubland bees, oscillating back and forth from exceedingly loud to completely silent in extraordinarily syncopated rhythm, chill him to his bones?

Johnny still worries about the condition of his grandfather. While Jimmy-Who-Knows' swelling has gone down, his face and body still look like an inflated balloon lying atop a pile of stuffed sausages. While some of Jimmy-Who-Knows' erratic breathing slowly returns to normal, it quickly slips back to fast, labored, gasping breaths again.

Twice Johnny has morphed into snake in order to sense the degree of infrared warmth emanating from his grandfather's body. Both times, he has been encouraged that his grandfather's red aura at least seems more intense and stable.

He estimates how long it has been since he has soaked a piece of cloth, ripped from Jimmy-Who-Knows' T-shirt, with some of the contents from the canteen...how long since he's dab-moistened the swollen parts of his grandfather's body.

It's not his determination that it's time to perform the hopefully healing ritual again that consciously transforms him back to his more convenient care-giver human form. It's the fact that his grandfather actually moans and moves.

"Grandfather?" Johnny tries to locate wherever it is that Jimmy's consciousness is. "It's Johnny. You've been pretty badly stung. I wasn't sure you were even going to make it."

He takes his grandfather's nearest hand and squeezes it. He waits for a response that doesn't...

The squeeze is returned.

146

Johnny is so overwhelmed with relief that his eyes tear.

"I came home to tell you something," Johnny says. If his grandfather apparently can't articulate words, Johnny is encouraged enough by the one-sided conversation to continue. "You weren't home. I came looking for you."

Jimmy's swollen bee-stung lips twitch but only emit another moan.

"I morphed at school today, granddad," Johnny confesses—it's something that still bothers him. "Once again, I couldn't control it. It happened on its own, right there in the hallway, in the proctor's chair. I had to get out of there as wolf, quick as blazes, before anyone saw me." Except, it hadn't been all that quickly, had it? "Luckily..."

Nothing lucky about it, and Johnny sees that quite clearly now. Whether his sudden insight is the result of his grandfather telepathically sending him information, or more likely Johnny's subconscious having finally rehashed the event sufficiently, the teenager now sees the potential magnitude for disaster in what has occurred.

The school has security cameras all over the place that have likely recorded everything that happened to Johnny in the school hallway.

#42 BEWARE, MAD DOG!

They must still labor under the premise that he only turns werewolf at the full of the moon. It must escape them that the power emanating from this place has screwed up a lot of things, including the normally scheduled transformations. Why else would they continue, so freely and so non-stop, to trespass on his territory and mark it as if it were their own?

Frankly, he's getting tired of their impertinence and is out to do something to express his dismay. He isn't referring to another follow-along squirt of his scent to mask theirs, either. He's tried that. It isn't working. It's time to make a bolder statement about how their audaciousness is no longer going to be tolerated or go unpunished.

All of these incomers, and there are more each day...all of those currently thinking of incoming (and he can hear them shuffling restlessly on the sidelines in his mind)...need to be taught a lesson that announces firmly and loudly, "Stay Out of Here, or You'll Bloody Well Regret It!" emphasizing "Bloody."

Where are they coming from, anyway? Who are they? What are they? It's like a macabre migration of beasties not content to stay put but, rather, as a mindless mass, intent upon intruding into his space to interfere with his peace of mind. Stupid, the whole lot of them, if they think he's going to let them get away with it forever and ever, amen.

Now, if he could only find one. So many here for not one to be seen. Maybe it means they know more about his evolving habits and routine than he's giving them credit for. Then, again, maybe it just means that he has to look a little more carefully in order to...

Ah! What do we have here?

Something to eat? Something to be eaten? Something looking to be eaten looking for something to be eaten?

Something that Matty, the werewolf, can accept? Something alien to the area that Matty, the werewolf, can simply not abide?

His question is answered by a miniscule shift of the existing, admittedly minor, breeze. Downwind from his prey, Matty detects the decidedly goaty aroma of the thing in the rocks across the way. Not exactly the most appetizing of smells, but nothing says Matty has to stick around, deed done, to dine. Merely making the thing dead—and what in the heck is it anyway?—will be message enough. The last thing Matty wants is more of these foul-smelling what-evers turning up on his doorstep.

He stalks it. He's good at stalking. In fact, he's

very good at stalking. Hardly ever does what he's stalking know it's being stalked until the stalking is over and done.

Finally, he gets a look.

Yikes! Anyone who thinks a werewolf is an anomaly of nature should get a good look at this monstrosity! Head of a lion? Tail of a...snake? The in-between torso, smelly goat.

Admittedly, it comes off a little more dangerous than Matty anticipated. That snaky tail looks like it might likely bite. Does it have venom? And those feline teeth look sharp, indeed, although they're presently occupied eating something—Matty can't tell just what —that should more likely be on Matty's supper plate.

He decides to strike while the gluttonous thing is occupied. This is Matty's territory, and Matty means to keep it that way.

Matty's success is aided and abetted by his leap upon the thing from higher ground. His lupine weight flattens the beast like a pancake. The thingee's tail whips uncontrollably. Whack—thwack!—its snaky head strikes against a boulder, which puts the secondary, and yes, fang-filled mouth out of commission. Matty bites down on the exposed nape of the neck and—crunch—wallah!—the spine snaps, and the goaty-smelling thingee is dead. Just like that.

He's congratulating himself on a job well done when he realizes from the fleshy debris scattered around him that what the thing has been eating was a man.

#43 NOW, I LAY ME DOWN TO

The candle blazes brightly, preheating the hardened wax cupped just below the flame, preparing the wax for its journey into the ether and beyond, while within the flame...

Kevin Chou awakens but continues dreaming— again. He's been in bed for an hour and a half; he dreams of being asleep, but he's not.

But how can he know?

When he opens his eyes, he sees his bed. He sees himself in it.

He sees moonlight flickering against one familiar wall because of interference from a wind-blown curtain.

He looks left. There's a poster of Bruce Lee. He looks right. There's a poster of the rock group "Emperor Ming." He looks down. Beyond his supine body, over his feet and the foot of his bed, there's his desk with his neatly stacked books, his homework to one side, complete and ready to turn in tomorrow.

When he shuts his eyes, however, even for a moment, he's once again flying.

He's above familiar terrain, known to him from awake-dreams several times before. No need for plane, or helicopter, or hot-air balloon, either. He has big, scaly wings.

Below, in every direction, is high desert with cliff-ringed reservoirs, rugged canyons with steep walls cut into lava that erupted through the earth's crust millions of years ago. Mineral lakes dot the horizon. He instinctively knows there are caves, even though he can't see any. And then there's the immense, dry waterfall in the distance that dominates the landscape.

Obviously, he's flying over central Washington state scablands. He's seeing them, though, from a different perspective than Kevin sees them each and every day, at ground level, where they're only barely noticeable beyond the perimeters of the ever expanding town of Flicker.

He sees sagebrush, Indian Ricegrass, Pinegrass, Broadleaf Cattail...

A straight-A student, and a whiz at biology when flying or not flying, Kevin identifies the more difficult Heartleaf Arnica, Wooly Milk-Vetch, Rabbithead Balsamorhiza...

This should be high adventure, a golden

opportunity to explore, but in actuality, Kevin is less into discovery than in determined flight—from whatever is in pursuit.

He's totally intent upon getting away. To where, he's not sure. Just away. He doesn't want to be found. He doesn't want to be caught.

Safety isn't all that far away, but he doesn't know where or how far way.

He's being continually harassed by a vicious pair of soul-mated hawks. They dive-bomb him continually, sometimes irritatingly scraping him with their talons. It's as if they suspect his primary purpose is to rob their nest.

Kevin fears for his eyes with one hawk always so close.

He blows on the offending bird to put it off track.

The hawk's feathers smoke, burst into fire, and disintegrate, dropping the bird like a rock, leaving behind a smell of roasted flesh, like Christmas turkey crispy-skinned, fresh from the oven. The roasted fowl's confused companion barely avoids a similar fate by diving in quick pursuit of what's left of its mate.

Kevin groans in genuine distress and opens his eyes—to bed, posters, desk, books—to completed homework.

He wouldn't purposely hurt a flea. He still gets

teary-eyed when remembering the day Qwinkee, his pet cockatoo, suddenly died over two years ago. Kevin had wrapped the bird in an expensive linen hanky, made a coffin, dug a grave, read a Buddhist text for his pet. Yet what had he just done...without feeling or remorse to the dreamt—real?—hawk-mate?

In the bedroom next to Kevin, Qwan Chou hears the restlessness of his teenage son and not only knows, but summarily fears, what Kevin's awake-dreams likely signify.

#44 SCREENS, ROOMS, HALLS, AND...

The candle-reading going on within the flame is as much a diversion for the Remoths as an information search. Concentrating on the green candle's flame doesn't entirely mask the sadness and misery of Trish's life prematurely taken. It does, however, somehow make the welling emotions manageable, so they don't spill over and flood each and every mental nook and cranny. It's just too easy to be consumed by the trauma of someone so young dying without something, anything, to detour the mind from fixating on the horror.

For Timothy, there's a definite need to get to the

bottom of what happened. He's curious, having received word from the downed pine that it wasn't responsible for Trish's death. If true, then, what did she die of? A heart attack? More and more young people seem to be dying from them these days. An aneurysm? Some people are born with weak blood vessels in their brains programmed to burst, at predetermined times unknown to the victim, time bombs genetically implanted before birth. Though a dedicated team of medical people will likely flesh out one of these possibilities as the cause of Trish's sudden demise, Timothy suspects it won't happen for awhile. If answers are available, they're needed now.

There's also the definite possibility that the shape-shifter, now identified as Johnny-Three-Spirits, is somehow responsible. The question as to why he wouldn't have killed Trish when first he had her at his mercy out in the scablands makes the possibility less likely, but... Do shape-shifters even have the capacity to kill via long distance? Not that the impossible remains such these days. Never before has Timothy communicated with a plant. And not just Timothy, but the others sitting at the dining-room table—Mr. and Mrs. Remoth and their daughter, Melissa—also sense the ongoing, changing dynamics of the power emanating from the very ground beneath their feet.

Things once normal are normal no longer.

When nothing results from peering into the flame, Melissa breaks, disappointed. She'd genuinely felt that something was in the offing.

"Your father and I may be the fault," Mary Remoth tells her daughter sadly. Obviously, she, too, is aware that they're making no progress. "Since he and I are so drained of our candle-reading abilities these days, we're possibly in some way plugging up the flow. Let your dad and I sit out for awhile."

"I think your mother may be right," Roger agrees with his wife. "I'm not even feeling a glimmer of anything."

"Are you sure?" Melissa is reluctant to let them go, even if they are impediments. They'll likely fixate on Trish's death, without the reading to occupy them. Melissa will still end up distracted.

"We'll be fine," Mary assures. "We'll be just over there." She nods toward the sofa.

"Timothy?" Melissa queries. She wonders if he, too, would prefer making a graceful exit. It's not as if he counted upon any of this when Melissa and he decided to hook up.

Timothy checks his watch. The time is later than he thought, but not all that much later. It's not as if Gregory Ranlin has ever set a curfew after which

Timothy had to be in bed, or else.

"Sure," Timothy says. "Let's give it another go."

The next thing Melissa remembers is her father shaking her and calling her name.

"What?" She seems wrapped momentarily within a lifting fog.

"What did you see?" he asks her.

Did she see anything?

"Melissa?" her mother stands beside her. She, too, looks expectant.

Yes, Melissa did see something.

"Screens," she says. "Screens. And halls. And rooms."

She doesn't say what else she saw. Possibly, she's said too much already. She's not really sure she wants Timothy carrying back a report of her full vision, and what it may mean, to the vampire and the Michaels brothers at the Ranlin mansion.

#45 RETURN TO THE SCENE?

"You have to remove the school's surveillance tapes," Jimmy-Who-Knows tells his grandson. It's the first complete sentence the man has managed since Johnny's doctoring has slowly, but surely, brought the older Indian around. Even then, it takes Johnny a good deal of concentrated effort to figure out what the mumbling means.

Anyone who sees Jimmy would likely comment upon his continued swollen condition. Johnny can recall, though, how much more swollen his grandfather had been short hours before.

"Until the tapes are destroyed, you are in grave danger," Jimmy points out the obvious.

"What with the earthquake and all, they may have been overlooked, or even damaged in the shuffle," Johnny hopes. "No one really monitors the screens anyway. The tapes are re-taped over after a couple of days. They're only there should an incident warrant their viewing."

"We should be so lucky," Jimmy says, and then adds, "but we'll deal with what we have to. It's not your fault that your body seems so determined to throw you off with untimely conversions to your other selves."

"I couldn't leave you here anyway, grandfather," Johnny insists. Strange vibes are in the air. Doesn't his grandfather sense them? Doesn't his grandfather hear them? Doesn't his grandfather smell them? The night has been filled with strangeness. Johnny is sure he's heard more than one scream—by what, he's still uncertain. He does know that whatever the unseen beasties afoot within the surrounding scrublands are, they might very well have no qualms about taking advantage of an old Indian shaman, low on magic, weakened further by scrubland-bee stings.

"You must leave me here," Jimmy insists. "The sooner you can get the tapes out of the security room and in our hands, never to be seen, the better it is for us."

"This place is dangerous even if you had your full wits about you, grandfather," Johnny insists.

Jimmy laughs. "Grandson, I have been part of this 'dangerous' landscape ever since I was born. I have survived it this long. I will survive it, alone, a few hours more."

"You don't feel it, then?" Johnny asks. Obviously, his grandfather's magic is almost gone, in that the eeriness of the air is almost palatable.

"Oh!" Jimmy says as if finally realizing what Johnny is telling him. "I see. Still, danger or not, we must make compromises. You can't stay here with me until morning, and I doubt I'll be able to move, or be moved, very far any time before that. The best time to get the tapes is as soon as possible. So, help me into the cave."

"What cave?" The only cave of which Johnny is aware is the small crevice in which the bees, still performing their on-and-off buzzing chorus, are temporarily residing.

"Not far," Jimmy assures.

It turns out, though, to be not all that close, either. In the end, Johnny reverts to wolf and half-drags, half-carries his grandfather the remaining distance.

Exhausted by the ordeal, Jimmy still insists that Johnny go do what he has to do. "I'll be fine," Jimmy assures. "Magic or no magic, I have a few surprises for anyone or anything trying to do mischief to me."

Albeit reluctantly, Johnny is persuaded.

As wolf, he heads off at a fast clip for Flicker High.

Shortly, though, he stops dead in his tracks. He sniffs the air. His ears perk. Over by part of the fence that surrounds Rockpoint Air Force Base, there is a group of men in great confusion. He hears them noisily take to the rocks in a direction opposite to where Johnny has sequestered his grandfather.

Johnny, wolf, mollified, continues in the direction of Flicker and hurries off into a darkness growing thick as black molasses.

#46 WHAT'S FOR DINNER?

Roman Michaels tosses and turns. He kicks off his blanket. He pulls his blanket back in place. He rolls to his belly. He rolls to his back. He rolls to his side. He rolls back onto his back.

He stretches for his bedside light, clicks it on and sighs loudly. His head flops down hard against the pillow. He folds his hands beneath his head and stares at the ceiling.

He's decided it's time for him to get a steady girlfriend, and he's mentally going over the list of potential candidates. He's played the field throughout his school years—there were and are, after all, advantages to spreading around his goodness. Lately, though, he sees how content his brother is with Cooper Loor. Even Timothy has Melissa Remoth.

Roman has to admit that he's not just a little jealous of all of this happiness suddenly going around by way of everyone but him having found a perfect other half.

He has no doubt but that any girl would be happy to have him as a steady. He's at the tip-top of the Flicker High social totem pole. He's attractive. He's fun. He's charming. He's a gentleman—for the most part anyway. He's a jock. What's not to like? What's not to want?

His problem is deciding upon which girl to bestow his goodness—which girl would make *him* most happy as a steady. Some of the pretty ones he's dated have been real bores. Some of the interesting ones have been not-so-pretty. His final selection has to be somebody not only pretty but also not dumb as a stump. He can't go dump-diving for someone out of his social class, either. While just the fact that being his steady would elevate even bookworm Shelly Mackrel (of "Here comes fish!" fame) so fast and so high in the pecking order as to give her a nosebleed, it would put a lot of other noses out of joint. Roman has a reputation to uphold that doesn't include alienating high-born friends by blatantly expressing interest in some low-born girl.

Kitty Myers would be perfect, but she's already going with Daniel Crane. While Kitty could likely be persuaded to make the shift, Daniel is pretty popular in his own right and starting a feud with him wouldn't make for fun times. Roman is definitely in favor of fun times. "Coke break!" he says aloud, the thinking having made him thirsty.

Streaking out the door and for the stairs toward the kitchen, he passes his brother's room, and notices Sydney snoring contentedly. Probably dreaming about

Cooper. Timothy, though, isn't in his room. Probably still consoling Melissa over the death of her sister. If, as Roman has predicted, Trish Remoth is indeed dead. Certainly, all evidence points to her being such.

Downstairs, he heads into the kitchen, knowing the room's layout by heart, not bothering to click on a light.

At the refrigerator, he pulls open the door for one of the cold Cokes inside. The refrigerator lighting spreads out into the room to reveal Gregory slumped in a nearby chair.

"Jeez Pleez!" Roman exclaims. "You scared the you-know-what out of me."

"Then, you'd better get a mop, quick," Gregory makes an attempt at humor, although he's feeling anything but humorous at the moment.

"You look like crap!" Roman says, grabbing a Coke and popping the top.

Can in hand, he shuts the refrigerator door and heads for the nearest light switch. He clicks it on and takes another look at Gregory.

"You still look like crap!" he repeats. He tries to remember when he's last seen—if ever—Gregory looking quite so bedraggled.

"Compliments will get you nowhere," Gregory says. "You might try and remember that."

"Your evening meal put up resistance?" Roman asks, pulling out a kitchen chair to sit facing Gregory across the corner of the kitchen table.

"Let's just say that I'm still very, very hungry," Gregory says and grimaces, displaying his two, sharp, pointy canine teeth.

#47 ON A SESAME-SEED BUN

Roman knew this night would someday come. After all, he and Sydney had been living in the same house with a vampire. What were the odds of never becoming lunch and a vampire? Not very good. He'd suspected that it would happen from the day "Uncle" Gregory had taken the two kids literally under his wings. Roman and Sydney's parents had died in an Amtrak train wreck outside of Boulder, Colorado. At the time, both parents, it had turned out, had been regulars on Gregory's luncheon/dinner list of seven, numbers two and four, by way of his weekly grocery list.

"Have you decided to turn me, then?" Roman asks. He's pretty much prepared himself for the inevitability and isn't going to fight. What's the point? He's only slightly regretful that he'll now never be able to explore the pros and cons of a going-steady relationship.

"Get real!" Gregory says, although he sees, and regrets, where he might have given that impression. "All three of my wards are of far more value to me daylight-mingling with the powers in ascendency. By way of thanking me for not turning you, though, you might do me the favor of bringing the Remoth girl back to life."

"Trish?"

"She is the only dead Remoth sister, is she not?"

"I can see where you might want to get on the good side of Trish's candle-reading sister, but you and I both know Melissa isn't going to thank you. Your and my definition of 'brought back' isn't likely to be Trish's or Melissa's, is it?"

"Not brought back for Melissa. Rather, as a complication for Briana James and her father, both of whom have become insufferable. Can you imagine the trouble they'll have trying to explain a resurrected Trish hanging around their house? It would be nothing less than poetic justice."

"You're not serious?"

"Just think about it, will you? It might be amusing, and amusements are so hard to come by, these days."

Roman doesn't have a clue if Gregory is serious or merely playing with him. He still doesn't have a clue, either, as to why Gregory looks so disheveled. He takes a big swig of Coke from his neglected can.

"So, why are you looking like you're looking?" he asks, for not the first time. "And why so hungry when you've been out this evening?" If Roman were to guess, it would be his already offered suggestion that one of Gregory's regulars got tired of being a food source. Or, Gregory ran into some difficulty in recruiting someone new to fill the spot vacated by Gyle Gril going flambé.

"It may surprise you, in that it certainly surprises me, but when I say I'm hungry, I'm not referring to blood. I'm thinking along the lines of one of those hamburgers advertised as having two all-beef patties, lettuce, cheese, pickles, onions, and special sauce on a sesame seed bun. You know the one?"

"A Big Mac? At MacDonald's? Do they still make those? If they do, can your system actually digest solids?"

"I can't say as I've ever before had the desire to try," Gregory confesses. "What say you get dressed and go buy your uncle one? That MacDonald's over on Basalt Street has been broadcasting non-stop that it's now open twenty-four hours a day."

"How about I give Timothy a call and have him

166

buy you one on his way home from Melissa's?"

Gregory checks his watch and frowns.

"Looks as if I just might have to have a talk with Timothy as regards being home and in bed by eleven on school nights," he says. "In the meantime, do call him and tell him to come home—with only that one stop at MacDonald's between there and here. And, oh, yes, have him buy me some fries, too, while he's at it."

#48 NOT IN HIS OWN IMAGE

His parents asleep upstairs, Duoto Bata is in his pajamas, at the kitchen table. Laid out before him are a ball of twine, several twigs, and pieces of black cloth and gray. The official school colors of Flicker High School are black and gray.

When attending Jefferson Cleveland High School in Portland, Oregon, Duoto was one of the school's most accomplished jocks, one of the chief cocks of the walk, to be more precise. Granted, for all the hoopla about African-Americans participating in all of the CH sports programs, most of his black athlete brothers couldn't play ball for diddly-squat. That made Duoto's mediocre talents shine all the more, like diamonds in a field of coal. And since most of the CH white boys were no more athletically inclined than most of their dark-skinned peers, Duoto stood tall over them, too, even in the usually lily-white-boy dominated sport of wrestling.

Duoto is furious at his father for having moved to Flicker, in the middle of nowhere, to where Duoto is convinced every superior jock in the country must have recently migrated. Duoto's talent has faded from sparkly-brilliant to unnoticeably dim in the amount of time it has taken him to check out of CH, drive to Flicker, and check into FH. He's not a happy camper.

He's particularly angry at Flicker's Coach Waynright for being good enough at his job to know from the get-go that Duoto doesn't have even close to what it takes to fill the one vacant spot on the Flicker High wrestling team. At the moment, it makes no difference that the coach has neither mocked Duoto's talents, nor the lack thereof, nor made the teenager feel ridiculous for turning out. Actually, the coach was quite diplomatic, politely encouraging Duoto to practice a bit more and try out for the team again—next year. As if Waynright doesn't know that all the practice in the world isn't going to make Duoto any better than he already isn't.

Duoto's rationalization for not going after his father, making Coach Waynright suffer instead, is that a father is, after all, a father. Enough said. One doesn't hex one's own dad, even if he is responsible for the move that's causing Duoto's present assimilation difficulties. Besides, his dad truly believed that coming here would rejuvenate the man's voodoo powers that were strangely melting away. He'd conjured a vision, while still able to conjure visions, that this was the place to come. Wrong! If anything, Gualbo Bata's remaining powers were draining even faster now that they'd moved to Flicker.

On the other hand, the moment he'd entered the Flicker area, Duoto immediately sensed a sudden intensification of his own powers. Heretofore, his skills at African magic had been so insignificant that he'd had to decline when his dad offered to take him on as a voodoo sorcerer's apprentice. If what Duoto is up to now works, though, maybe he'll tell his dad he's changed his mind about that apprenticeship. Maybe he'll still be able to rescue some pointers from his old man before his dear dad's entire once-practiced but no-longer-working repertoire of voodoo magic is entirely lost.

He begins assembling twine, and twigs, and cloth into a representation of Coach Waynright. He even has some of Waynright's hair he's collected from the drain in the coach's private shower stall at school. No big deal in getting it. He'd just had to hang around, waiting for the opportunity, and then recovered the small hairball.

Duoto doesn't linger to admire his artistry, because he's even less of an artist than an apparent jock these days. It's the meaning behind the miniature doll that really counts anyway.

He picks up a pin from the table top and inserts it where the figurine's heart would be, if it had one.

A few miles away, Coach Waynright folds upward into a sudden sitting position in his bed, grabbing his chest, and crying out in pain.

#49 THE NIGHT HAS A THOUSAND EYES

The glowing flame, crowned with light, having worked its way half-way down the body of the candle, flickers momentarily, as if a cold draft passed icy fingers through its ethereal body. Deep inside the heart of the flame, the unreeling vision shifts.

Twice something very large has shuffled about just outside Jimmy-Who-Knows' cavern sanctuary. Twice the Indian has had to muster the physical and mental willpower to provide a warning growl of bear to warn off whomever, or whatever, might think the cleft in the rock safe and empty. Not easy for Jimmy to do, because his face and throat, even his vocal cords, are still bee-stung swollen.

He's having second thoughts about insisting that Johnny go. He's having second thoughts about having been so blasé in insisting that he can take care of himself. Obviously, his grandson is the one now more attuned to the spirit of this place. Obviously, his grandson is the one now more likely to judge better whether or not Jimmy is safe here or not.

If Jimmy didn't know there was so little vegetation in the scablands to burn, he'd suspect a raging fire outside was fast approaching. More than once in his life, he's heard the sounds of a massive exodus of wildlife, big and small, sounding very much like these, each time in the wake of a blazing wildfire.

Something outside is once again heard attempting to join him. Not so big this time, Jimmy thinks, that a bear sound is necessary to ward it off. Instead, he calls upon the more easily achieved hiss of snake. The would-be intruder has second thoughts and moves off amid the clatter of even more stones in slippery slide.

Wait, is that people he hears? Yes, people! Human voices shout back and forth to each other. Saying what? Jimmy hasn't a clue. It's muted and made indecipherable by the large expanse of space through which it must travel to reach him.

A search party, perhaps? Looking for him? Has Johnny so quickly reached the school and rounded up some assistance to rescue his grandfather from the cave in the scablands? Surely Johnny knows that Jimmy is in danger, no matter how much his grandfather professes that he can handle anything in so familiar terrain.

People...and...

Dogs. He hears their bark. And...

Helicopters! There's little chance of mistaking the distinctive thwack-thwack-thwack of rotary blades.

A police helicopter? Does the Flicker Police Department even have a helicopter?

A military helicopter? What are the odds that the Air Force has been called in to give assistance that includes air support?

Despite the continued foreground sounds of fleeing animals—there are still more than a few—none of the animals seem interested any longer in seeking asylum in Jimmy's cave. Though they are not as close now, the animal sounds are still closer than the background sound of people and shouts...than the dogs and the barks...than the helicopters with their thwack-thwack-thwacking blades beating the resisting desert air.

The background sounds suddenly stop progressing; the foreground sounds taper off and disappear completely.

Jimmy would call for help if he thought anyone would hear him. As it is, in spite of the nearness of the people, the dogs, and the helicopters, he hasn't the strength to muster a coherent call loud and long enough to bring them running.

The human sounds remain for a surprisingly long time within that just barely too-far distance for hailing. Doing what? Possibly it's some kind of military maneuver. Except as distant as it is, it isn't nearly distant enough to be within the fenced perimeters of Rockpoint Air Force Base, is it?

Then, the background sounds, like the foreground sounds earlier, recede, eventually disappearing entirely.

Strange! Even disturbing.

Not as disturbing, though, as the sudden shuffling at the cave entrance and the shadow suddenly blocking Jimmy's view of the blackness outside.

Jimmy growls as bear.

The unidentified creature turns and growls louder and longer in bone-chilling response.

#50 THROUGH THE EYE OF THE NEEDLE

The scene-in-candle-flame flutters and shifts, the

*former yielding to a newer, stronger, more steady
vision...*

None of the Flicker High School buildings have
apparently suffered major structural damage as a result
of the earthquake. Anyway, that's what a preliminary
examination of the premises shows immediately after
the earth shook, then shook again, then shook again. A
more thorough examination will have to be conducted
later. School, in the meantime, will be closed until the
final okay is given for students to return.

The three broken windows that resulted should
have helped Johnny-Three-Spirits, but they don't. Quite
the contrary. They are the cause, along with other minor
damage, for extra security being hired for the evening.
The principal, Mr. Farling, is well aware of what
mischief kids can get into, given a few hours of spare
time and half an opportunity, and he'll have none of it.

Luckily, Johnny doesn't have to rely upon his
human form to crawl through a well-guarded window,
or his wolf or cougar form to pick a way through the
shards of glass everywhere. He doesn't need a window
or a door—all doors into the building are most likely
locked anyway. He takes advantage of a small hole the
earthquake has conveniently provided between a bit of
damaged wall and foundation for snake to slither
through with relative ease.

Once inside, he reverts to human form and heads stealthily for the basement security room.

During any given school day, the room's bank of computer screens actively displays images of all rooms and hallways. There was initial debate about putting cameras in the bathrooms and locker rooms, Mr. Farling having come to Flicker High from an inner-city school in New York City. Based on his experience there, he tells the parents of Flicker High students that, if left unobserved in any room, students in general can be relied upon to be doing drugs, engaging in sex, and/or harassing each other, the rest malingering while waiting for an opportunity to join their colleagues. Flicker parents, however, seemingly more concerned with the prurient opportunities provided the viewers of any bathroom and locker-room scenes, squelched Mr. Farling's recommendation faster than he could raise it.

Every student at Flicker, Johnny no exception, knows where the security room is located, simply because it is off-limits to each and everyone of them, except during the one-time, mandatory, new student tour. The one and only walk-through is the proof Mr. Farling provides each potential mischief-maker that anything untoward that goes on within the walls of Flicker High is available for instant replay. Students had better watch their steps.

Although usually locked every evening, the security door opens easily for Johnny. Apparently, it — and quite likely other inside doors—has been left unsecured in the aftermath confusion of the earthquake and aftershocks. Apparently, it's assumed that locking all of the school's outside doors and providing a few walking guards inside are more than enough security for the moment—definitely a wrong assumption with Johnny-Three-Spirits on the prowl.

Inside the room, with the door pulled shut behind him, he goes to the consoles and searches for any tapes still in their recording slots. The door being unlocked, it hardly seems likely to Johnny that anyone would have yet gone to the bother of removing and filing the last tapes.

However, not one slot, but all slots are empty.

"Don't bother checking the files," a sudden voice from a darkened corner issues, scaring the living daylights out of him. "What we're looking for isn't here, either."

#51 CALL ME WHEN IT'S DINNER TIME

Timothy hands the MacDonald's bag off to Roman with a questioning look.

"It's not for me, buddy," Roman says and passes the bag on to Gregory.

"The whole town out of blood, is it?" Timothy asks. This can only be a practical joke, designed to re-emphasize Gregory's parental control of his sons. "Can a vampire even eat a hamburger and fries?"

"Or drink a Coke?" Roman says. "You didn't forget his Coke, did you?"

"What's everyone doing up at this time of the night?" Sydney asks from the kitchen door, rubbing his eyes with the backs of his hands, unable to suppress a yawn.

"What do you mean?" Roman asks, all innocence. "Gregory is up at this time every night."

"Funny!" Sydney says, making it sound otherwise.

"You looked like you were dreaming about you and your boyfriend, so we didn't want to disturb you," Roman says.

Sydney sees the hamburger, fries, and container of Coke that Gregory has un-bagged and lined up on the table in front of him. "I suppose no one thought to order me anything."

"You can eat whatever Gregory doesn't," Roman says.

"Gregory's eating? That? You're kidding, right?"

"Are you kidding, Gregory?" Roman wants to know.

"Flicker really all out of blood?" Sydney asks.

"That sounded funnier the first time, coming from Timothy," Roman says.

"And why are you looking like crap?" Sydney obviously refers to Gregory.

"That, too, has already been said...by me," Roman adds. "Apparently our mentor has had a very difficult night of it and has decided to drown his sorrows with a fast food junket."

"Should we get you a barf bucket, Gregory?" Sydney wonders aloud.

"Yeah, should we?" Roman echoes his brother's concern.

"How the hell do I know?" Gregory says. "It's not like I've had this urge to eat or drink anything but blood since I was turned—ever."

"The times, they certainly are a-changing," Sydney says.

"Not yet to the extent, however, that I condone any of my wards staying out all hours," Gregory says paternalistically. His accusatory stare nails Timothy to the spot. "The rule around here is, all boys in bed by eleven, on each and every school night, young man. Since this is the first time I've reminded you, and since, suddenly, there is no school tomorrow, we'll let it slide this time, but only this once."

"Sorry," Timothy says. "Melissa and her parents asked me to stick around and candle-read with them."

"Oh?" Gregory sounds as if Timothy's excuse just might be a valid one. "And...?"

"Her parents both bowed out, insisting that they no longer had the ability."

"Tell me about it!" Gregory says, stating a reality that pertains more and more to him, too, these days.

Timothy, though, takes him literally. "We were just sitting there, nothing happening, and Mrs. Remoth said she and her husband were likely the ones blocking the vibes...or something like that. They got up from the table and went to the couch. Melissa and I tried again, at which time, Melissa went all weird and kind of passed out on us."

"'Kind of passed out?'" Gregory's attention is no longer on the food in front of him.

"We all jumped up to catch her, because we thought for sure she was going to slide out of her chair and, well, because of Trish's death, you know. When Melissa came to, she said she'd had a vision...of screens, and rooms, and hallways."

Gregory waits for Timothy to continue. When the teenager doesn't, he says, "Which Melissa interpreted as meaning what?"

"None of us, including her, had a clue."

"You don't think maybe your girlfriend is holding out on you, do you?"

"Why would she?"

"Maybe because she knew you would report to me?"

"That's never kept her from being frank before."

"Hasn't it?"

"You think she's held back before, then?"

"We all hold some things back sometimes," Gregory observes. At least, that's how he's always found it, and he's been around a very...very...long...long...time.

"I'm not holding anything back," Timothy insists.

"Well, I suppose there's always a pleasant exception to the rule," Gregory grants as he picks up the hamburger sandwich, opens his mouth wide, and takes a very large bite of it.

#52 THE TAPE HAS LEFT THE BUILDING

"Melissa Remoth, right?" Of course, it's Melissa Remoth, but to say that Johnny is thrown for a loop by her being there, in the security room with him, at this very moment, is the understatement of this year and the next.

"Johnny-Three-Spirits, right?" Melissa answers back. Of course, it's Johnny-Three-Spirits, just as her last candle reading said it would be. "Or, should I call you Johnny Wolf, Johnny Cougar, or Johnny-Snake-After-The-Tape?"

"What tape?" he asks, deceptively.

Melissa frowns. Of course, she frowns. Does he think she's an idiot? Why else would he be in the security room of Flicker High, after midnight, except for the tape, just like she's there for the same tape. Nonetheless, if he wants her to confirm what he already knows...

"The tape that shows my sister's confrontation with you—where she identifies you as her kidnapper. Where you do whatever it is that you did to see her drop dead a few hours ago."

His reply is spontaneous and filled with shock, "Your sister is dead?"

"Now, why does it surprise me that you seem so surprised?"

"Maybe because I *am* surprised. Surely, you don't think I killed her?"

"If it looks like a duck, walks like a duck, and quacks like a duck, I'm inclined to believe it's a duck.

According to my parents, the only two things Trish kept raving on about when she got home from school yesterday was you, and how she'd found you out."

"All my grandfather and I wanted was a little information about the girl in blue."

"So, you say, but how did you even know about the girl in blue?"

"My grandfather saw her and you, together, vaguely, in one of his last vision-dreams, before he stopped having them. It concerned him, since an Indian maiden, in blue-dyed buffalo skin, is renowned in my people's history for appearing just before major disasters."

"I've never met the girl in question, but what I candle-read of her says she isn't Native American and I don't think her robe is dyed buffalo skin, either."

"Nonetheless, there are a lot of strange things going on around here, lately, or haven't you noticed: Timothy Gril's dad burning up in that fire. The earthquake. Your sister dead. And how about people, like my grandfather, masters of magic for years, losing all of their abilities? While, coincidentally, I seem to have so much Magic streaming through me that I can't control it. That's why I grabbed your sister, instead of you, at Dry Wash Gulch. That's why I bit her, as snake, when I only wanted to carry her somewhere private for a harmless talk. It was, by the way, just such an uncontrollable transformation by me to snake, cougar, and wolf, right in a school hallway yesterday, that has me so anxious to get hold of the tape that recorded it. I'm not here, afraid it'll show something I did to your sister to make her die."

Melissa is inclined to believe him. She was inclined even before he showed up. Sixth sense? Something within the same candle-read that correctly predicted him here, now? Why else did she come here all alone, without back up, when he could certainly kill her just as easily in his guise of snake, or cougar, wolf, or even as Johnny-Three-Spirits, as he could have killed her sister?

"You might take lessons from Timothy Gril in the art of simply asking for information," Melissa says.

"Is it true the Gril kid's mentor, Gregory Ranlin, is a vampire?"

"So, it would seem," Melissa says. "See how easy asking and getting an answer really is?"

Johnny offered his only valid excuse: "Native Americans, considering our history, are less likely to trust than you might be. Untold information of great value is often not easily surrendered."

Which is exactly why Melissa keeps a few secrets of her own, although it's not just to maintain secrets that she isn't telling them, here and now. It's the sudden muffled sound somewhere in the outside hallway that causes her and Johnny to go instantly silent.

#53 OF GRAY CONCERN

Sydney makes a bee-line for the pantry and brings back a mop bucket. He stands at the ready.

Roman and Timothy stare fascinated as Gregory consumes his first bite, and then a second, of the sandwich in his hands.

"Mmmmmm, mmmmmm good!" Gregory says between chews.

"You seem to have a Big Mac confused with Campbell's soup," Sydney tries for levity, expecting Gregory to upchuck at any minute.

Seconds pass, then minutes.

Gregory finger-feeds himself some fries.

Third bite of sandwich, second bit of fries, are all washed down with a large swig of Coke from the container.

"Didn't anyone ever teach you boys that it's rude to stare?" Gregory says, and then pauses long enough to wipe his greasy lips with one of the several napkins the clerk at MacDonald's conveniently provided.

"How do you feel?" Roman wants to know.

"I feel as if I'm being stared at by a trio of peeping Toms, none of whom is named Tom," Gregory says. "Why don't you young ones go to bed and let your elder sit here and finish this delicious meal in peace? I can hardly remember the last time I had anything to eat and drink but blood."

"We're not going anywhere," Sydney says. He's still expecting Gregory to turn green at any minute and pay the consequences for breaking a few hundred years of liquid fast.

Gregory takes another bite of sandwich, chews, says, "Okay, then, Sydney and Timothy, let's use our quality time together to persuade Roman to work his magic and bring Trish Remoth back to life as soon as she's conveniently available in her grave."

"Bring her back to life?" Even believing simultaneously in vampires, candle- and card-readers, diviners, shape-shifters, maybe even werewolves, and sporting the ability to converse with tree spirits, there are still some things in the universe Timothy isn't quite yet able to accept as possible.

"I'm figuring to have him do it as a bit of aggravation for the James girl and her wretched father," Gregory says. "Roman is resisting."

"By all means, bring her back," Timothy says.

He's thinking of Melissa and her parents.

"It's not exactly how it sounds," Roman argues. "Does the word 'zombie' bring anything to mind?"

"You'd bring her back as a zombie?" Timothy, like Roman, is no longer convinced it's a good idea.

Gregory, though, following another bite of sandwich, is prepared to continue arguing in favor. "Roman needs some practice in raising the dead. When was your last zombie, my boy? Use your talent, or lose it, as they say."

"Who are they?" Roman wants to know.

"Your mentor, your brother, and Timothy, here, for three."

"I don't think so," Timothy has already opted out.

"Oh, don't be such party-poopers!" Gregory insists, finishing off the last of his sandwich.

Leaving a few of the fries, he proceeds to wipe his hands again but suddenly stops.

"What?" the three boys ask in unison, anticipating the worst from the indefinable expression on Gregory's face.

"Is this actually a gray hair?" Gregory asks. Perplexed, using the long fingernail of his right index finger, he pinpoints the white strand definitely rooted on his left knuckle.

#54 THE KEY PART OF THE PUZZLE

"I think it was just the building doing a bit more settling after the quake," Johnny says with finality.

"I think you're right," Melissa agrees. Anyway, she hopes their combined intuition is honed enough to weed out real from imagined danger.

"I suppose you haven't a clue as to who got to the tape before we did?" Johnny wonders aloud.

"You're right, I haven't a clue. A candle reading might provide some insight, but I don't see any candles, let alone the right one."

"A correct candle makes all the difference, does it?"

"One way to make sure some everyday person doesn't have my kind of success by just grabbing any old wax-wrapped wick off some novelty-store shelf."

"What kind of reading do you think you could manage from a candle of scrubland bees' golden wax?"

"What's a scrubland bee?"

"The little monsters that stung my poor grandfather senseless while he was trying to liberate their hive of the necessary wax and honey. Which reminds me that I need to get back to him soon. I left him so that I could get in and out of here before the inspectors turned up."

187

"Sorry about your grandfather."

"He was out for the ingredients to make a candle, of course. He wanted to call you in to do the reading. Think you can be persuaded?"

"You think he'd actually try hive-robbing again after being stung so badly the last time?"

"I'll be doing the collecting this time."

"And what makes you think you're likely to fare any better?"

"It's a matter of scrubland bees respecting possessors of Magic," Johnny says, having concluded it after-the-event. "They sensed my grandfather no longer has it. In me, they sense something else again."

"Amen, to that," Melissa says with a smile, "at least as regards you definitely being something else again. Even I sense that."

"You feel it, too, then, Melissa? The draining of whatever power your elders once had while yours gets bigger and stronger by the moment?"

"Mmmmm." She nods agreement.

"Do you have a clue what it all means?"

"None, except that it has something to do with the girl in blue, and the questions we need to ask her."

"You think she actually exists, then, outside the world of dreams and visions?"

"Oh, she exists, all right. Not that far away,

either."

"You think?"

Melissa wonders if she hasn't just let go a little more valuable information than she should have.

"It's a good possibility, don't you think?" she gives him that much.

"I really have to go."

"Actually, I do, too," Melissa says.

"Have your escape route figured out?"

"Same way out as in. Can't be simpler than that."

"That reminds me—how did you get in?" Suddenly, he knows how she got in. "Oh, that's right, your father's company was in charge of construction, wasn't it? Bet he has door keys still lying around."

"And alarm codes. Meaning, I guess, that magic isn't the only way to achieve one's objective. I try not to forget."

"Darn, I never even thought of alarms."

"Oh, oh! That means you likely tripped one on the way in. Except that the police would have surely been here by now."

"I entered as snake, through a hole in the wall."

"Darn clever of you; darn lucky for us!" Melissa is impressed. "Well, I can provide us a more convenient exit than that."

Johnny follows her out of the room.

One of the building's interior shadows suddenly stops moving when Melissa and Johnny enter the hallway.

#55 I AM SHADOW, FOR NOW

As soon as Melissa and Johnny pass, the shadow slides from the school-hall wall and assumes human form.

His constant need to remain cloaked these last few days leaves him exhausted. It requires all his concentration. He was, in fact, on the verge of completely losing it when the two teenagers finally exited the building.

His problem is opposite that of the young shape-shifter, Johnny-Three-Spirits, who has too much power to control. The power in the area is always on the verge of controlling Johnny, sometimes even succeeding. That's what Shadow decided yesterday when, clinging to the corners of an alcove, he saw Johnny go from snake, to cougar, to wolf, before finally managing a frantic and unseemly exit before anyone but Shadow and a security camera saw what happened. Shadow's opinion hasn't changed.

All of which bodes ill for Shadow and his ilk. He

doesn't fear for his kind in general, who will somehow undoubtedly survive. He fears for the subsection that includes the likes of him and others who are out of their teens and already into adulthood or even entering old age.

A group of his peers sent him to the school to reconnoiter. With their power seriously on the ebb elsewhere in the world, rumor is that Flicker, Washington, is perhaps the last watering hole—or fueling depot, so to speak—where anyone with Magic in decline can go for a fill-up.

The rumor, however, is wrong. To that, Shadow can bear personal witness.

Quite the opposite, this environment, even now, is an ever-increasingly stronger vacuum seemingly intent upon sucking from him, harder and faster, what little of his black powers still remain. And, if his observations are correct, will likely re-channel what is rightfully his into someone far younger and far less deserving. The power elite in Flicker are obviously its teens. Since kids from other areas of the country don't seem to be benefiting from the magic drain of their elders, something is going to have to be done before the teens in Flicker are the sole possessors of Magic, leaving everyone else, young and old, at their mercy.

Maybe the group Shadow represents will be able,

in their waning moments, to conjure some answers and even a solution. Definitely, the group will have to recruit some easily-manipulated teenagers and stick them within the Flicker environment to benefit from it. Who cares how much Magic such pawns soak up as long as Shadow and the other members of his group remain the ones moving them on the playing board? The very idea of being at the mercy of someone as goody-goody naive as Johnny-Three-Spirits, who doesn't even understand his own inherent power, gives Shadow genuine chills. The very idea of being at the mercy of others like Johnny-Three-Spirits, should the teens ever figure out what is going on, turns Shadow so cold that touching him would freeze fingers.

For now, he has to report back. Plans have to be drawn up to locate Shadow and his allies at the advantage. If everyone in Flicker, including its teens, is presently running around without a clue, then alliances between the teens must already be forming and broader alliances between those with waning powers will be essential. Too many new alliances made by the former, and Shadow and his faction may well find it too late to control anything that goes on. Shadow has enjoyed secretly exercising black magic for so long that he won't stand for it being passed on to anyone he doesn't control. And he knows more oldies but still goodies (or, rather, baddies), who, like him, feel exactly the same way.

#56 KNOCK, KNOCK! WHO'S THERE?

Wax flows, like hot, boiling lava; the flame, sputtering, wanes weak, suddenly drained of fuel and color. The vision inside, rich, robust, three-dimensional a moment before, shrinks, hesitates, as if deciding whether to flee or remain.

Frightened big time, Jimmy-Who-Knows voices his bear growl, again. It comes out a pitiful moan, again. His breathing is raspy. Whether in response to the monster at his door, or a belated allergic reaction to his bee stings, he doesn't know. He struggles to his feet, but despite his best efforts fails at assuming a defensive posture. Unable to defend himself, he realizes that he isn't going anywhere, either. Overdosed so recently on scrubland-bee venom, his body is still shut down, swollen and lethargic.

"Hey, mister, calm down!" Matty says, morphing from werewolf to teenager with far greater ease than he'd thought possible. He hopes the darkness masked the change. Always, in the past, he's had to maintain his werewolf form until dawn. No if's, and's or but's. Yet, at this moment, there's not even a hint of daylight on the horizon.

The man in the cave, whoever he is, looks as if he's having trouble seeing, even breathing. His eyes have obviously been swollen, appearing at the moment like large, dried prunes.

"Whatever that thing was, mister, it's gone."

Matty, werewolf, had been running scared, ever since he spotted the body on which the dead goaty "something" had been feasting when he'd killed it. Matty makes it a point to dine only on local wildlife and on occasional stray livestock. Humans are not on his menu, no matter how tempting. Human remains bring in search parties, and police, and dogs, and guns. The proof of that is how the military has appeared, as if by sixth sense. Strange, in that the dead man wasn't wearing a uniform and wasn't found on the military base. Of course, the victim could have been killed on the base and dragged the distance. Over the high, chain-link fence with barbed wire coiled along its top?

Matty had had to get the heck out of there.

The sounds of approaching helicopters, and knowing that they might have infrared-detection equipment on board, decided that he would have to find shelter within the first available rock-shielding hole. If he hadn't been running scared, he would have known the cave was occupied before stepping into it.

"Who the heck are you?" Matty drops to his knees and tries to get a closer look at the cowering man. "You look like you're in bad shape," he says to the man and to himself.

"Who are you?" Jimmy wants to know. He wishes it wasn't so dark. He wishes his eyes weren't so swollen. He wishes it to be Johnny, knowing from the voice it isn't. The kid actually looks somehow familiar. *What was that—thing?* He really wants to know and ask, but he doesn't, at least for the moment. If he didn't already know that his senses were likely playing tricks on him, he would have thought the one was, also, the other. Another teenage shape-shifter? Can't be! Despite his almost total loss of power, he still should be able to recognize another shape-shifter. Besides, no way could the monster he'd seen been the result of shape-shifting. The thing had been too grotesque, and hairy, and human, and lupine. A werewolf? Not all that long ago, Jimmy, who had never seen a werewolf, would have nevertheless recognized one, and its host, in his presence. But not any longer.

"Looked like a big wolf," Matty says. No way is he giving his name. Next he'd be asked to explain what he's doing out here, in the middle of nowhere, in the dead of night, hiding from a wolf, corpse, and the military.

"Take it from me who knows, that was not just a big wolf," Jimmy argues.

"So, what happened to you?" Matty asks, wanting to lead the conversation off the subject of wolves, which might evolve to include werewolves.

"I was stung by bees. My nephew has gone for help."

"Your nephew?"

"Johnny-Three-Spirits."

"Ah!"

"You know Johnny?"

Another question Matty has no intention of answering.

In fact, now that he knows someone is already out to get help for this bee-swollen man, Matty's one and only desire is to get as far away as possible from Johnny-Three-Spirits' uncle and from the military contingent that might still be searching outside.

#57 WHAT THE EARLY BIRD CATCHES

Cooper hears the phone ring in his parents' bedroom. He can't hear the other side of the phone conversation, but it's easy enough to guess what it's all about.

They need Lt. Col. Loo back at the base. Now. There's a problem. Can he please return ASAP?

Cooper doesn't know the specifics, but he's been aware for awhile it was in the offing. He's intuited that it won't be short-lived, either. That's why he made a point of enjoying the quality time spent with his father the night before. It would be awhile before his dad could manage a repeat performance. There's absolutely nothing Madison or Cooper or Mrs. Loo can do about it. It's time to roll with the punches.

In emphasis, Cooper rolls away to the far side of his bed. Actually, he's just trying to get more comfortable. No need to worry about the time, or about getting up, since there's no school today. Inspectors are scheduled this morning to certify the earthquake damage to the new school buildings. Actually, all the damage seemed minor, leaving Cooper to believe there'll be school as originally scheduled tomorrow, leaving him safe for a prolonged sleep-in today. Still, he's determined not to go back under before his father stops in to say good-bye.

Irrespective, he's soundly asleep, though, when Madison walks in, sits the edge of the bed, and smoothes some tousled locks from his son's deeply tanned forehead.

Cooper sleepily opens his eyes and gives his father his best it-isn't-your-fault smile. "Taskmasters calling you back to the treadmill?" Cooper asks. He stretches and makes a couple of his vertebrae crack.

"I'll try to be home early again tonight," Madison says.

Cooper knows better, but he doesn't say so. Instead, he says, "I hope you're not being summoned so early because of some major catastrophe."

"Major enough so that they don't want to discuss it on an open line," Madison says. It's more information than he usually gives.

"Mom and I will keep the home fires burning," Cooper promises.

"Love you." His father rumples Cooper's hair by way of final good bye, gets up, and leaves the room.

Cooper snuggles in to get better nested between blankets, sheets, and mattress. He falls back asleep for another couple of hours.

This time, it's his phone that wakes him. If the school prohibits cell phones, his cell phone is his constant companion during any off-time, including bed time.

It's Sydney. "Rise and shine, handsome."

"What time is it?" Cooper shifts to check his bedside clock and groans at the, in his mind, still-early hour. "Jeez, Sydney, this is a no-school day. We get to sleep in."

"So, has anyone told you yet that Coach Waynright is in the hospital?"

Cooper sits up straight. "From what?"

"Nothing more than a bad case of indigestion, it would seem. Painful enough, though, that a call was made to 911, an ambulance and fire truck and paramedics rushed on the scene, and the man taken to the hospital, siren wailing. They kept him overnight. Guess he and his wife thought he might be going to meet his maker. For which, I'd never have forgiven him, considering we're scheduled to wrestle the regional champions next week."

Sydney breaks off momentarily to say something to someone (his brother?). Whoever it is says something back. "Holy Moly!" Sydney says, still off-line. Then, to Cooper, "Give me a quick minute, here, stud."

Cooper returns to a more lie-down position in his bed. As soon as Sydney gets around to ringing off, there'll be more minutes of sleep time on Cooper's early-morning agenda.

"Hey!" Sydney's back. "You want to head on over here and see what a vampire looks like alive and well in the full light of day?"

#58 IT'S THE BAGGIE MAN

Although he was up for a big chunk of the night, Duoto didn't sleep well once he crawled into bed. He kept beating himself up for having wasted so much time and effort with the voodoo doll of Coach Waynright, only to have changed his mind at the last minute. Oh, he'd stuck the pin into the chest, but he'd pulled it out just as quickly. In the end, he felt he shouldn't have been seeking revenge on Waynright, who was merely doing what any coach does: doing what's best for his team. Duoto had known that from the get-go, but he'd also needed to vent his frustration, and the coach had just been handy. Spending half the night conjuring a voodoo doll had proved an effective way of venting, even if it did come to nothing in the end.

His hard-won, fitful sleep is interrupted by his mother opening his bedroom door and checking on him before she and his dad head out for the hospital.

"You awake?" she asks softly.

"I'm awake."

"We're leaving now."

"Bye."

"You're still going to join us for breakfast in the cafeteria?"

Is he? He's tired. He needs more sleep. He wants

to sleep long enough so that he doesn't end up feeling yet again like a fish out of water in this ho-dunk little town in the middle of nowhere. Yet, how can he explain any sudden decision to beg off? Just come right out and say, "Sorry, mom, but I've been up all night trying to hex Coach Waynright, and I need to catch up on my sleep"? Nah! His mother's grandmother was supposedly killed by voodoo, and Ruby Bata would not be happy to hear about her son messing around with the dark side. Suspecting his mother had never really been all that comfortable with her husband's magical skills, Duoto wonders if she isn't actually pleased that Gualbo's voodoo is on the ebb, even if she did willingly agree to join him in Flicker-in-the-middle-of-nowhere, Washington.

"Ruby!" his father calls from downstairs. "We're going to be late!"

"I'm coming!" she hollers back, signing off with Duoto by saying, "So, we'll see you around eight, then?"

She's taken the decision out of his hands. He will have to get up soon to join them for breakfast in the hospital cafeteria. This, in the end, is okay, because he suspects he won't be getting any more sleep anyway. His mind is racing to figure out how to dispose of the doll. He'll have to check with his dad, if his dad hasn't already forgotten how a destruct is done. Life is just so darned complicated!

He dozes on and off until he finally hauls his weary self out of bed to shower, dress, and head on out. It's not a long walk, but he gives himself plenty of time. He needs to figure out how he's going to fit in around here, especially if he can't rely on voodoo or athletics. So much of his time and effort has been spent these last few days trying to figure out how to fit in. How come people couldn't automatically fit in everywhere, saving folks like him all the bother?

His temporary solution for disposing of the doll is to seal it in a baggy and put it in his pants pocket, in case he has a few minutes alone with his father at breakfast. His mother would be less understanding of Duoto's conjuring act in the kitchen while she was sleeping. She's never had any trouble fitting in anywhere. His father, on the other hand, has always been a nerd and remains one even now. How Duoto's father and mother ever got together has to be the prime example of opposites attracting. That they're both mainstream physicians had to have helped their relationship, in that they'd always had plenty professional to talk about.

His dad, already sitting at a table, waves to get Duoto's attention. Duoto waves back and then goes through the service line, deciding on scrambled eggs, bacon, an English muffin, and a glass of milk.

"So, where's mom?" he asks, sitting across from Dr. Gualbo Bata, M.D.

"Discharging Coach Waynright," Gualbo says, hungrily wolfing down hash browns that look a disgustingly long ways from crispy.

"Coach Waynright from Flicker High?" As if there is some other Coach Waynright and some other high school in this cow-pie-on-the-road town. Duoto feels nervous. He's actually afraid to ask why the coach is checked in.

His father fills in the blank without being asked, "Thought he was having a heart attack, but it seems to have just been indigestion."

Duoto wonders if now would be a good time to fish the voodoo doll out of his pants and fill in his father on a few things that likely won't make his dad happy. Then again...

Gualbo's phone rings, putting Duoto's decision on hold.

"Darn!" Gualbo says into the mouthpiece and slips his cell phone back into his white hospital jacket. "It seems your mom won't be joining us, after all. Coach Waynright has developed a serious breathing problem."

Duoto silently mouths a dirty word which neither his mother nor his father would approve. By way of verification, Gualbo gives his son a chastising glare over the top of silver, wire-rimmed glasses.

Hurriedly, Duoto fishes the small doll from his pocket and clumsily breaks the seal to give the damnable thing some air.

#59 IN WHAT WATER?

Lt. Col. Madison Loo paces the floor between the two temporary tables set up in Hanger 214-B. The building is located as far as possible from any of the Rockpoint Air Force Base's perimeter fences. At the moment, the base has the potential of becoming at least as infamous, if not more so, than Roswell's fabled Hanger 18.

"Let me get this right, if I can." Madison has an audience of two. They are the base's Commanding Officer, Colonel Jeremiah Growlan, and a "Mr. Smith," in sunglasses and a dark non-descript suit, rank undetermined. The latter, who works for a government agency of which Madison has never heard, somehow managed to arrive on the scene even before Madison. "This..." Madison pauses, not quite sure what to call the occupant of the table on his right. "...thing," he decides finally and whacks an unoccupied section of the table with the palm of one hand, "was videotaped committing a murder."

"We'll show you the video when we're finished here," Col. Growlan promises.

Without turning to look, Madison whacks an unoccupied section of the adjacent table with his other hand. "The civilian victim, here, one Peter McGee, is/ was a professional photographer, scheduled to have a major exhibition in a prominent Seattle art gallery next Sunday."

"Correct," Col. Growlan affirms. Mr. Smith nods in agreement.

"Mr. McGee was killed off-base, just outside the perimeter fence."

"Correct," Col. Growlan affirms. Mr. Smith nods minimally in agreement.

"Mr. McGee, and this...thing...that killed him, were pursued by our airmen, only to be found dead and brought back here."

"Correct," Col. Growlan affirms. Mr. Smith nods minimally in additional agreement.

"Which I'm supposed to help cover up?"

"Correct," Col. Growlan affirms. Mr. Smith nods more firmly this time.

"Because the thing that killed Mr. McGee might —just might—be the result of the local water supply having become contaminated by a botched biological warfare experiment conducted on this site in the nineteen-sixties?" Madison still isn't at all sure he has this part right.

"The area in question was capped by four feet of concrete," Mr. Smith says, "which we just finished determining remains viably intact to this day. What might have happened, however, is that an earth movement or movements, some time in the past— similar to what occurred here yesterday—cracked the underlying bedrock through which the contaminated water, under pressure, flowed into the aquifer up north. That would account for the sudden abundance of water around here. Drainage from the aquifer up north may well now be flowing back beneath the contaminated area which, until now, had, quite frankly, been forgotten."

Madison, at a complete loss for words, can only shake his head. Finally, though, thinking of his wife and son, he says, "Which means we're all bloody exposed, and must be assumed capable of mutating into circus freaks like this thing!" It's not a question, although his follow-up is. "Don't you think it would be more responsible to warn the people in Flicker of the danger lurking in their water supply?"

"Except that we don't know for sure, yet, that the drinking water is actually contaminated," Col. Growlan reminds. "So far, it's only *suggested*. Until we can be sure, it would be irresponsible for us to raise a false alarm that would only cause unnecessary panic," adding with emphasized finality, "and a likely irreversible public-relations disaster."

#60 READY, AIM, FIRE!

"Sit down, Kevin," Qwan Chou instructs his son. "We have to discuss this dream of yours which is—tell me if I'm wrong—occurring more and more frequently."

"It's just a dream, pops," Kevin argues.

"Unless it isn't just a dream," Qwan Chou says cryptically.

"Whoa!" Kevin responds, wondering from where that wild ball came.

"Do, please, sit," Qwan instructs. "This is of utmost importance."

Kevin sits. Qwan sits in the chair directly opposite.

"What are we talking, here, if not a dream?" is

what Kevin now wants to know.

Qwan pauses. This is a subject he's hoped he'd never have to discuss with his son, or anyone, for that matter. Just their luck, or lack thereof, that of all places in the world, the Chou family had to put down roots in this town. Then, again, there was the rumor that Qwan Chou's family always carried around the potential for just such moments like this and historically had to deal with them, from time to time. Qwan Chou just wishes it wasn't Kevin and he who have to deal with this one.

Qwan takes a deep breath and says, "There was a time when all in our family were dragons."

"Right, pops!" Kevin says, making it sound, "I think not!"

"In ancient China, Twock Pow Province to be exact, across the Xalin Mountains from Tibet," Qwan says, "we killed off everyone and everything else in the area and then went looking farther afield. In the process, we inadvertently stumbled across the geographical boundaries beyond which we were dragons no longer."

"Come on! You can't be serious!"

"Just be quiet and listen, please."

"It's just been awhile since you told me a fairy tale."

"You'll not think it's a fairy tale when you start

sprouting scales and foot-long claws," Qwan says.

"This isn't Twock Pow Province, or mythical times," Kevin reminds. "This is Flicker, Washington. Twenty-first century."

"Most of our family enjoyed the transformation to human and stayed outside the Twock Pow boundaries. Those who remained, eventually, for want of anything else to do, killed off each other, leaving the last dragon to die of old age."

"Oh, pops, be serious!" Kevin protests.

"Certain rare power-spots, like Twock Pow, it turns out, exist worldwide to this day, providing the circumstances for our re-conversion to dragons. We try to avoid these places."

"Let me guess...the area around Flicker just happens to be one of them."

"Do you want to wait around to find out?"

Kevin will have to think long and hard about that one. Quite frankly, he could think of more than a couple of his fellow classmates at Flicker High School who he'd personally enjoy turning into crispy-critters.

"How about you, pops?" Kevin says. "You sporting scales?"

"Surprisingly enough, no."

"So, maybe, it's just a dream I'm dreaming, after all."

"Nonetheless, I'm sending you to San Francisco to stay with your grandparents until I can make arrangements for your mother and me to join you."

Quite suddenly, Kevin's neck and head go dragonesque. His newly coalesced reptilian mouth, lined with double rows of large, sharp teeth, opens wide.

"I'm...not...going...anywhere!" he says in a bass voice that shakes the house on its foundations more violently than the recent earthquake and aftershocks had done.

He breathes a jet of fire that shoots the length of the room, singeing Qwan Chou's hair in passing, and lights the sofa on fire. "Ah, so," Qwan Chou replies, shaking his head sadly from side to side.

#61 BLOOD AND CHOCOLATE

Gregory climbs awkwardly through the open window and sits, exhausted, in the chair next to the bed. It's becoming more and more difficult for him to fly. Being airborne takes more time, effort, and concentration these days; so much so that he almost didn't make it through the window. In the end, he does, hoping for some normalcy to a life which is increasingly topsy-turvy.

How ironic that the normalcy he so desperately wants, now, isn't at all the same as the normalcy he wanted when he first became a vampire. Back then, suddenly forced to rely entirely on blood meals for sustenance, he desperately longed for a return to regular food. Now, it just seems plain weird that he's somehow being weaned from that very blood which has been his sole life-source for several hundred years.

He looks at the woman on the bed. Rhoda Wesmore is twenty-six, very pretty, the very bud of physical health and perfection, all from maintaining a natural diet and good exercise. She teaches yoga twice a week, cardio-vascular routines three times a week, and is a personal trainer at the local gym.

There was a time when Gregory would have preferentially feasted on the blood of any and all such athletes as a way to assure his own continued well-being. He'd been wrong, of course. In recent times, even well-respected athletes shot up steroids in order to bulk-up, and Gregory had found himself as negatively affected by those drugs as the ones who took them. He became stressed out: moody and sullen, short on temper and quick to anger, but equally addicted to the intravenous drugs. How many members of the Russian sports facility in Vladivostok had he sucked dry in his mad craving for more and more tainted athletic blood? So many had been converted by him to vampirism, they had run out of new blood in the athletic complex and had turned on each other to feed. What a mess that had been! The local authorities, unable to cope, had called in the military. The one positive thing that came out of the debacle was that Gregory realized he needed more control *over* his life, and more stability *in* it, than steroid-laced blood allowed. Oh, but how unpleasant the withdrawal had been. How very, very much so.

Since then, he came to look upon blood like Rhoda's as much healthier and nutritious. In addition, he'd introduced her to Xoçai Chocolate, which elevated her blood to that of a gourmet dessert. After she partook of that mixture of antioxidant-rich açai berry and dark cacao, Gregory, from first suck, knew her blood was something above and beyond all the regulars upon whom he had feasted. Meaning, if he isn't feeling tempted to drink Rhoda's blood now—and he isn't— that whatever strangeness is happening within him is so profound as to quite likely be permanent.

Lying quietly on her bed, the smells of her Xoçai-chocolate breath invite him to, once again, partake. The large vein in her sexy, bare throat is pulsing in open invitation for his canine teeth to dig in and enjoy.

Instead, he gets up, goes into the living room and

then into the kitchen, where he begins blindly opening and shutting cabinet doors until he locates her personal cache of Xoçai chocolates—two boxes—XoBiotic Squares, dark chocolate with açai and blueberry; and Xoçai MEGA Squares, dark chocolate with açai and orange—that she keeps in reserve. He unwraps a square and pops it into his mouth, followed immediately by another. And another.

He can hardly believe the ecstasy from the undiluted-by-blood flavor as it suddenly explodes upon his tongue and slides sensuously the length of his throat into his belly.

He's licking his fingers and still tasting the wondrous aftermath of the healthy confection later that night, at home in his own living room, in his own easy chair, when Timothy comes in carrying a package and drops it in his lap.

"A gift to you from Melissa," Timothy says, by way of explanation. "She was inspired by a dream and says you'll understand."

The quickly discarded tissue reveals a rich, satiny-appearing, dark-brown candle, dribbled with brilliant red, orange, and blue wax, all smelling deliciously of...Xoçai chocolate.

#62 HOW WOULD YOU LIKE YOUR STEAK?

"Come on in, Cooper," Timothy says from the other side of the opened mansion door. "Sydney's in the bathroom primping, and says to tell you that he'll be with you in a minute." He takes a formal step back and waves in the direction of several chairs. "Roman is off doing whatever it is Roman does. At the moment, I think he's trying to decide what lucky girl to make his steady for the rest of the year. And I'm off to meet with Melissa Remoth to tell her sister's boyfriend that his girlfriend is dead."

"Don't envy you your task," Cooper says and means it, heading for the nearest chair.

Timothy leaves by the front door.

True to his word, Sydney joins Cooper within the minute. He's all smiles.

"They say miracles no longer happen," he says, as his arms enfold Cooper who stands to meet him. He gives his combination guest and boyfriend a long, intimate hug. "Hmmmmmm, you feel so good!" He follows up with a kiss. "And taste even better."

"Neither of those is, of course, the miracle to which you refer."

"Come," Sydney insists. "You really do have to see this. It's genuinely unbelievable!"

He takes Cooper's hand and leads him through the labyrinth of rooms to the sunroom whose large floor-to-ceiling windows open onto the expansive backyard.

Gregory sits on a lounge chair, reading the morning newspaper, popping a Xoçai chocolate into his mouth every so often. He looks up.

"Didn't someone recently tell you that it's impolite to stare?" He smiles.

It's the first time Cooper has seen him in daylight. It's the first time Cooper has seen him without fangs.

"Shouldn't you be snap-crackle-and-popping in all of that sunlight?" Truly, Cooper is amazed.

"You would think so, wouldn't you?" Gregory says. "I woke up this morning—unusual in itself—and had this uncontrollable impulse to step into natural sunlight. Pretty much like last night when I had a helpless urge for a hamburger and some fries."

"You're not feeling sick?"

"Neither sick nor sunburned, it would seem," Sydney answers for his guardian. "What he is feeling is a little bit older than usual. He has a gray hair. On his left knuckle. Go ahead, Gregory. Show him.

"Have I now become some kind of exotic exhibit in our own little zoo?" Purposely, Gregory cups his right hand over the top of his left. "If I have, shouldn't you be paying admission to see me?"

"Come on, Gregory," Sydney cajoles. "Maybe our diviner, here, has some suggestions regarding what's going on."

"Believe me when I say that I haven't a clue," Cooper says.

Nonetheless, Gregory unveils the knuckles of his left hand and extends his fingers as if he's a dowager empress expecting them to be kissed.

"That hair is definitely gray all right," Cooper confirms. "Maybe, it's even white."

"Isn't it, though?" Sydney agrees.

"Meaning what, do you think?" Cooper asks. Since he doesn't have a clue, he wonders if maybe one of them, despite all indications to the contrary, might.

"It means that Gregory isn't a vampire anymore, right, Gregory?"

"You're human, again?" Cooper exclaims.

"I think not exactly human...not yet," Gregory vacillates. "At the moment, I suspect I'm somewhere between human and vampire, moment-by-moment leaning more towards the human."

"And beginning to age like one, too," Sydney points out. "Let's hope he doesn't reach his real age within the next few seconds, like in those vampire movies. Otherwise, we'll be left to sweep up his dust-residue."

"Nice!" Gregory says, but he makes it sound anything but. "Such a little wise-ass. I definitely should have turned you while I had the chance."

"Too late now, it would seem. Na-na-na, na-na-na!"

"I still have a few things I can do that..."

Gregory stops mid-sentence, an absolutely horrifying look of painful anguish sweeping across his face. His eyes go wide. His mouth gapes. He pants low and loud.

"What?" Sydney and Cooper chime in unison.

"I'm suddenly feeling so hot!" Gregory screams.

"Get out of the bloody sunshine!" Timothy demands.

"Too late!" Gregory proclaims.

"My God, I think he may be spontaneously combusting—from the inside-out!" yells Cooper.

#63 REDEFINING THE FOOD CHAIN

"Good grief!" Lt. Col. Madison Loo exclaims even before the video has played through. He has an almost uncontrollable urge to pick up the nearest telephone, and order his wife and son to drink nothing but imported bottled water from here on out. "What is that...thing?" Not the first time the question has been asked, nor the last time it will be asked by him or by others.

"You tell us, and we'll all know," Mr. Smith says emotionlessly.

On the computer screen, the chimera fastens its lion's fangs into the back of Peter McGee's neck and lugs the dead man into the landscape off range of the camera mounted on the air base's 24/7-bugged perimeter fence.

"It looks like a lion," Madison says.

"It looks like a snake," Mr. Smith says.

"I'd say it kind of looks like a goat in its midsection," Col. Growlan says.

"What do the medical people say?"

"We're having a special team flown in," Mr. Smith says. "We can't trust this to anyone without a security clearance far higher than anyone in the medical department here has."

"If it mutated...from what did it mutate?" Madison would like to know. "From a lion? We don't have any big-mane lions in the U.S. outside of circuses and zoos. Any escaped in this area, over the last few years?"

No one answers.

"Maybe it mutated from an indigenous snake," Mr. Smith suggests.

"Maybe from some local's stray goat, by the looks of its midsection," Col. Growlan ventures.

The video continues playing, showing only the usual bleak landscape while a series of grunts, snarls, hisses, bleats and groans ensues.

"There are going to be queries as regards Peter McGee." Madison is making a statement, not asking a question. "McGee is not some vagrant who wandered into the scrublands looking for a lie-down. He's a well-known, well-respected photographer scheduled for a major exhibition at which he's definitely going to be a no-show. If anyone has any clues as to where he went to shoot these last pictures, and I suspect they do, they and the press are going to be all over this area like bees over clover."

"We've been very thorough in covering our trail," Col. Growlan assures. "We've become expert at doing that over the years, as you well know."

"McGee's body *not* found would make everybody even more curious," Madison predicts. "Reporters will soon be digging up incidents of locals reporting livestock dead by mysterious circumstances."

"What's mysterious about wolves?" Col. Growlan asks.

"Better a curious public, than one presented with the evidence of Mr. McGee's gruesomely mutilated remains," Mr. Smith reminds.

"Are we sure there were no witnesses, other than this video, to the murder, or to the arrival of our airmen to haul away the pieces of the man and the body of the mutant monster?"

"Who would possibly have any reason to be out in the scablands at that time of the evening?" Col. Growlan asks.

"Besides a photographer taking pictures?" Madison tries to cue them in to the odds.

"No one else was spotted," Col. Growlan assures.

"Well, let's pray to God that continues to be the case, or we're going to end up between a rock and a hard place."

"People disappear all the time, and for no apparent reason," Mr. Smith reminds. "More than a few of those missing are likely just as important, if not more so, than our Mr. McGee here."

"So, would either of you like to venture a guess...." Madison is thinking about the search parties that he expects will soon be turned loose in the surrounding area. "...as to what is still out there that is big enough, and strong enough, to have taken on this mutated monstrosity and ripped out a large chunk of its throat?"

#64 CAUSE FOR A PINNING

"I say, again, not funny!" Sydney complains loudly. "Not funny at all."

"Gregory attempting another of his not-so-funny jokes?" Roman asks from one doorway of the sunroom.

"Gregory was pretending he was on fire, spontaneously combusting in the sunlight from the inside-out," Cooper explains.

"Scared the crap out of me..." Sydney says, looking none too happy. Gregory cut in. "I probably did it because Sydney was getting aren't-I-the-funny-guy kudos by complaining of the mess he'd have to clean up if I suddenly reached maturity in a matter of seconds. It was like being in one of those staked-through-the-heart vampire horror movies. Definitely not something to joke about in the presence of a vampire losing his powers..."

"Do you have any powers left at all?" Sydney interrupts.

"...and with very little else to take Mr. Smarty Pants down a peg or two other than a bit of play-acting," Gregory concludes. "Actually, I was on the stage, and quite successful, I might add, during one phase of my very long life."

"I didn't say anything about actually wanting you

to dissolve into dust," Sydney reminds.

"Well, let's just call ourselves even, then, shall we?" Gregory decides. "Although I suspect Mr. Loor, here, will now expect that I owe him one."

"Damn right!" Cooper agrees. Actually he's not thinking any such thing, but having Gregory in his debt, even if the man's one-time vampire powers are on the ebb, or even completely gone, can't be a bad thing.

"And what brings you to our little party, Roman?" Gregory asks, settling back onto the chaise longue and reaching for another Xoçai chocolate from the small, glass-topped table close by. "Since you don't have any friends in tow, I presume it's not to gawk and marvel at the anomaly I've become."

"I'll bet he's here to announce the selection of the lucky girl who's soon going to be Mr. Top of the Heap, Head of the Class, Super-Jock Extraordinaire, the one, the only, Roman Michaels' steady girl friend," Sydney suggests. He follows up with some obnoxious vocals that are supposed to be a trumpet fanfare.

"You've decided on the lucky girl, have you, Roman?" Gregory asks. He's been so long out of school that he more often than not forgets how important such things as who is dating whom, where, when, and why, can be to a teen. How tiring it is to have all of those hormones rushing helter-skelter through a body not yet used to them. Frankly, Gregory is glad to have all that far behind him. He'd take back any one of his lost powers of vampirism before he'd want to return to even one day spent trying to adjust to puberty.

"As a matter of fact, I'm thinking of Tania Quilnox," Roman admits. "She's from a socially prominent Flicker family, she's pretty, she has a sense of humor, she's on the cheerleading squad, and she has more than average intelligence. And she's available."

"You left out that she's a friend of Briana James," Sydney reminds.

Roman tries to decide whether or not his brother is purposely out to make trouble.

"Briana James is on Gregory's let's-dump-on-them list, if you remember correctly," Sydney continues.

Roman is now certain his brother is trying to make trouble.

"Actually, it's her father who's presently at the very top of that list," Gregory corrects. He's still smarting from Nalbot James's laughter when Gregory literally fell out of the man's first-floor window. "Let me think on how your dating a friend of his daughter might be of any benefit to him."

"Briana being Briana, it'll be pretty much impossible for me to find someone acceptable who isn't her friend," Roman argues.

"Mmmmmmm," Gregory doesn't sound convinced.

"Besides, by way of payback for whatever it is that the dad and daughter have done to offend you, Gregory, I'm thinking I might just go ahead and bring Trish Remoth back to life. Just to complicate theirs."

Gregory smiles widely, revealing startlingly white teeth and normal canines.

"Promise to do that, and keep to that promise, my boy," Gregory says, "and I might very well be the one to personally hand over your social-club pin to the lucky Miss Quilnox for you."

#65 DO WHAT TO THE MESSENGERS?

The candle flame suddenly burns steady and bright; images project sharp and movie-like on the interior flame and seemingly come to life.

Timothy automatically takes Melissa's hand.

"How are you holding up?" he asks, giving her fingers a squeeze.

"Certainly better than my parents. They were already depressed because of the drain on their magic. I'm afraid Trish's death has sent them rock bottom. My increased powers, on the other hand, seem to be helping me cope."

"You're sure you're up to telling Trish's boyfriend? I could do it for you."

"You're sweet," Melissa says and returns his firm grip to show her appreciation and growing affection. "But I'd better be the one to tell him. He's almost part of the family, after all. He and my sister were actually talking marriage."

"How do you think he's going to handle it?"

"Not at all well, I suspect, and that doesn't make me any more eager to break the news, either. My doing the deed, though, is far better than him hearing it from someone else."

They turn into the walkway and make it to the Donnelly's front door. Melissa rings the bell. They wait.

Mrs. Donnelly answers.

"For goodness, sake, look who's here! How long has it been, Melissa Remoth? Ages! And how's your mother, these days? She and I don't talk nearly as often as we used to, though, I guess, with a possible wedding in the offing, we'll be getting back to regular chit-chats any day now, won't we?"

"Do you know Timothy Gril, Mrs. Donnelly?" Melissa doesn't want to go down the road Mrs. Donnelly is presently leading. Let Matty deal with telling his mother and his father.

"Gril? Gril? Oh, dear!" Mrs. Donnelly's face registers genuine compassion. "Not the boy whose...?" She leaves the sentence hanging.

"We're here to see Matty, Mrs. Donnelly." Whichever way the conversation has veered, it still isn't where either Melissa or Timothy wants it to go.

"Message from your sister, honey?" Mrs. Donnelly is as thankful for the shift in conversation as Melissa is. The poor Gril boy's father, after all, was burned to an unimaginable crisp.

Melissa tries to decide how to answer Mrs. Donnelly when the woman makes the decision unnecessary with, "Matty is out back in the shed, tinkering with that trail bike of his. Something to do with a broken sprocket—whatever a sprocket is. If it even is a sprocket. If it isn't, though, I wonder how I ever came to think of such a thing. Actually, though, I do believe he said it was the chain that needed fixing, or changing, or..." She looks dazed, and then shrugs. "Just go on around back. You can't miss him. He's the one making all the noise. It was very nice to meet you, Timothy."

Melissa and Timothy take the cobblestone pathway around the side of the house.

Face the backyard, and Matty's noise-making

226

becomes more evident, emerging from the shed, door open, across the lawn.

Melissa takes an audibly deep in-draw of breath.

"Ready, set, go," she says, and they step forward in unison.

They march up to and into the shed.

Matty looks up from his bike that's turned up-side down and supported by its seat and handlebars.

"Melissa?"

No difficulty in interpreting Matty's additional look over and beyond the two teenagers as an attempt to spot Trish somewhere in the background.

"I'm afraid I have bad news, Matty," Melissa says. "I'm afraid it's really bad." No need to prolong the inevitable, Matty already looking grief-stricken in mere anticipation of what's about to come. "I'm afraid Trish died last night."

"Died?" If Melissa thought she was seeing grief before, she's suddenly seeing it ten-fold. "Died?" he repeats, obviously disbelieving. "How can that be?"

"We're not sure how or why, and we won't know anything more until the doctor's report is back. It was all very sudden and unexpected."

Matty is so filled with anguish, so consumed by despair, that he turns werewolf, right then and there. What's more, he is fully prepared to repeat the habit of despots, everywhere, who spontaneously kill the bearers of bad news.

#66 POT CALLING THE KETTLE BLACK

At the hospital, and feeling guilty, Duoto stops in to see Coach Waynright who is, "Feeling better, kid, thank you." Actually, Coach seems genuinely appreciative that Duoto is there. "Don't know what in the heck is up with me, lately. The doctors don't seem to know diddly-squat, either."

After which, snooty Miss Briana James and a few of her nose-in-the-air fellow cheerleaders sashay into the room to purr their condolences. Duoto makes a quick exit. During which, he experiences "it."

It is something he's long heard about, but has never known anyone actually to have. Certainly, it's something he's never personally known before.

His by-pass of Miss Briana James somehow manages to spark one of those mysterious connections between sorcerers that includes more than just an exchange of glances (and chilly ones at best). Duoto is suddenly bestowed with the knowledge that the bitch is not only a witch but is harboring one mighty big secret to boot.

He waits away from her eyes in the lounge area, panting, wondering if she, too, feels what passed between them.

Sure enough, a few minutes later, she reappears, alone, from the coach's room. She spots him, where he stands, and heads over like a cat that just swallowed a canary.

"Who would have guessed the new black boy is a warlock?" she says. "Certainly, I wouldn't have."

"Not exactly a warlock, Little Missy White-As-A-Corpse Witchy-Woo," Duoto corrects. "Voodoo priest would be a far better definition."

"Who would have guessed you to be a voodoo priest?" she says. "Certainly, I wouldn't have."

"Who would have guessed a bubblehead like you to be a witch," Duoto tosses right back at her. "Certainly, I wouldn't have."

She frowns.

"Bit of a hypocrite, aren't you?" she says. Her catty smile is back. Her eyes suddenly look downright evil. "I mean, first putting the coach in the hospital, and then stopping on by to suck-up?"

"Says you."

"Ah, well, I'm the witch who knows." Her smile goes big grin, but displays no warmth. It is all Cheshire-cat from "Alice in Wonderland."

Duoto does not like this babe at all. All of the vibes emanating from her—and there are a whole slew —are black as coal and negative, negative, negative.

"Well, despite all you know, you still look like a dumb bubblehead."

This doesn't please Briana at all. She frowns and quickly becomes someone not very pretty. Obviously, this dame thinks she's someone, something, special. Well, to some people she very well might be. To Duoto —nope!

"What do you think would happen if I let it get around that you were an African Mumbo-Jumbo Boy so angry at the coach for keeping you off the wrestling team that you poked pins in his image? Where is the little doll, by the way? Still in your pants? Or, is your warlock—oops, your voodoo priest daddy—taking care of it for you? If he is, you should have second thoughts. The old folk these days don't seem to be very good at holding onto their power around Flicker."

"Well, firstly, what would happen," Duoto says— this admittedly frightening babe might scare others, but she doesn't scare him—"is that I'd have to say that my ancestors are more immediately from Haiti than from Africa. Secondly, I'd have to say that I didn't use pins, only one pin."

"I don't much like your attitude," she says.

"Well, tough turkey! I don't much care for yours, either, so we're even."

"We'll see," she says, obviously in threat mode, "what the wrestling team has to say about its coach being laid up when there's an important match scheduled for just next week."

Does this babe think that the lightening-like exchange that occurred between them is some kind of one-way street? If so, knowing otherwise is to his advantage, and she's in for a mighty big surprise.

"We'll see what everyone says when they learn that you and two of your witchy friends killed Trish Remoth."

From her surprised expression—dropped jaw, mouth agape, eyes wide—he realizes he's just told her something that he's somehow plucked from seemingly thin air and about which she didn't have a clue. Interesting. Decidedly interesting.

#67 BUG-EYED

Uxana hoped to be more rested this morning, but she's wearier than she was the day before. The night was full of things and their sounds, all of which constantly disturbed and, in the end, made her more fearful. Worse yet, she was physically cold the whole while. She's still cold. Candlelight provides little true warmth. Without her robe, she would be frozen solid and awaiting thaw despite a sunrise well above the horizon.

She sits cross-legged on icy-feeling stone, looking at her purple creation.

Such a wretched piece of workmanship! Of all the candles she has ever seen, this one looks least likely to perform magic, let alone the high degree of Magic that'll soon be demanded of it.

She goes over in her mind, for not the first time, the instructions her mentor and fellow Sister in the Sisterhood, Zila, mentally imparted to her before suiciding. So much information transmitted at such breakneck speed, Uxana remains concerned that she might not have received it all, or received incorrectly what she did receive.

All it takes is one mistake in the prescribed chain of ritual for a procedure to fail. Nor can a wrong, once done, likely be righted, what with all information sources except Uxana, and the one she would now attempt to summon, dead and gone.

Nonetheless, succeed or fail, she has to get a move on. She's too long ignored that time is of the essence. Real disaster looms, if whatever is happening to put the world out of whack isn't put right again and soon. Last night is proof-positive of that, filled as it was to the brim with things that shouldn't have been there. What's more, Uxana senses that the beasties are gaining, not losing, dominion.

Okay, then, enough procrastination! Time to do what has to be done, come what may.

First, she performs a final mental rundown of what must occur. In the end, two things absolutely must be accomplished, though just one thing would be more than too much to expect of so pathetic a candle. Two things? Hopeless! Hopeless!

She tries to clear her mind. She needs all of her wits about her.

She closes her eyes and commences slow and even breathing. She focuses her concentration. She anticipates just the right moment to ignite the wick and begin, in earnest, the first of two necessary rituals.

She begins a slowly cadenced countdown from five to four to three to two to..."

She's interrupted.

Her night having been filled with strange and eerie sounds, her day now explodes with one more of the same.

She stumbles to her feet. Her twist toward the cave entrance sends her blue robe into a swirl that tips the purple candle, flinging wax against the rocky floor and causing the candle to become even more misshapen.

Whatever is making this new, horrible sound is close. Very close. And it's getting closer.

She goes to stand just inside the cave's entrance, looking out and down over its lip. Nothing.

Then, it appears. Not at ground level, but in the air.

A dragon? No, not a dragon! Rather, a grossly formed insect, projecting thwack-thwack-thwacking noises in every direction; a threatening-looking bug with a single, enormously monstrous eye that catches and casts sunlight into Uxana's place in the shadows, leaving the lone Sister of the Sisterhood painfully exposed, unable to move, completely blind as to its intentions.

#68 DID YOU SEE WHAT I SAW?

"Grandfather," he calls, "it's Johnny!"

"I better get in there," the medic insists.

"You might want to let me go first," Johnny warns.

Unable to land on such irregular terrain, the

medical-rescue helicopter hovers above its suspended lifeline.

"My grandfather may be old, but if he still has his wits about him, he can have you down and dead before I can do anything about it."

Thwack-thwack-thwack go the rotors slicing the morning air.

"Just give me one minute," Johnny says, jumping from the hovering craft and heading into the cave.

He's wary. While he knows the importance of hurrying to get his grandfather medical assistance, he has to be careful these days.

"Come on, grandfather," Johnny says. "I've a medic, as well as a helicopter, to take you to the hospital."

In his heart, he's afraid the old man is dead. Who knows what all that bee venom had done to his grandfather's nervous system?

Further, Johnny worries about having left the old man on his own, especially since the attempted retrieval of the tape from the school security room proved a complete fiasco.

"Grandfather?"

Maybe Jimmy-Who-Knows isn't even here any more. Maybe he's wandered off. Maybe an animal came in and carried him out and off. Worse...

"Are you the werewolf, come back to take me?" a weak and pitiful voice queries from the shadows.

"Grandfather, it's Johnny!"

"Johnny, or the werewolf out to fool me, again? It was very clever of you to manage a conversion to human form in the dead of night. Can such a thing happen in these strange times? Can you, like some empowered shape-shifter, convert to a replica of my grandson, even now, with full day outside, as the whim strikes you? Is that, too, now possible?"

"It's me, grandfather," Johnny insists and finally manages to see far enough into the shadows to recognize the small figure huddled in its tight ball against the back wall of the cave."

"Johnny?"

"My grandfather is over here!" Johnny summons the medic already on his way in and probing the darkness with a flashlight. Kneeling beside his grandfather, Johnny finds his grandfather looking a little less worse for the wear, possibly less swollen than when he left him.

"You were right when you said he'd been stung!" the medic says, joining them. He rifles through his medical bag for a blood-pressure cuff. "Here, hold my flashlight, kid, will you?"

Johnny does as instructed.

"Did I tell you I was visited by a werewolf?" Jimmy says, staring into the dark space around them.

"Right, grandpa." Johnny makes it sound as if he thinks Jimmy's ramblings are untrue, though he does believe them.

"Darned ugly. Darned big," Jimmy says, sounding more present. "Did you even know we had one in the area?"

Oh, yes, Johnny has smelled its urine and spotted patches of its fur snagged on thorns of bramble bushes. Would he admit as much in the presence of the medic? No way!

"He's one of your classmates at Flicker," Jimmy says. "I've seen him at ball games."

Johnny can't help wondering which classmate. Food for thought. One of many questions for later.

"Your grandfather's blood pressure is pretty low," the medic says, removing the stethoscope from his ears and releasing the Velcro, with a loud ripping sound, that secures the cuff. "His heartbeat is weak and fluttery. We have to get him to the hoist and to the hospital."

"We're going to put you into a harness that'll lift you into the chopper, grandfather," Johnny says assisting the medic in wrestling the old man to his feet. Supporting him, they begin their walk towards daylight. "Just see if you can manage the few steps necessary.

You can do that, can't you?"

It's not easy but is finally achieved. The two affix a harness about the old man, and clip the harness onto the hoist snap-hook. The medic grabs the steel line and rides up with the old man to unload him at the top. He sends the cable back for Johnny. As soon as the teen is safely on board, the chopper veers back the way it came.

Uxana hears the return of the monstrous insect that moments ago had, for some inexplicable reason, simply ignored and passed her. Perhaps it has reconsidered. She watches its approach, this time shielding her eyes lest its monstrous, light-reflecting, evil eye blind her again. The horrendous bug seems close enough to reach out and grab her.

Twack-twack-thwack!

In sudden recoil, she steps back and directly onto her purple candle.

She scrambles for it in the darkness, surprised, when she no sooner has hold of it that its wick spontaneously ignites.

Whether she's ready to proceed or not, it's prepared to do whatever it can before she accidently destroys it completely.

#69 FULL METAL JACKET

"Who would have expected?" Timothy refers to Matty's sudden, fierce and aggressive conversion to werewolf, in full light of day, right there in the shed, right in front of their eyes. "Wonder how he managed it?"

"Wonder how you managed to provide such excellent interference?" Melissa congratulates. She refers to the way the bike became airborne, inserting itself in between the changed Matty and his intended victims, and then contorted to wrap the poised werewolf in a spider webbing of twisted and curved steel that fully encases his torso and now weighs him down on the floor. Matty-werewolf tries vigorously, but futilely, to get free. "I don't think that's something Matty did. Certainly, it's nothing I could have managed."

"I'm not really sure how I did it," Timothy confesses. His ability to move, bend, twist, and contort metal, obviously getting more and more advanced, still has him frankly in awe. He merely knows, the minute Matty unexpectedly converted to werewolf, something had to be done, if Melissa and Timothy were going to live to tell the tale.

"Did you know that your one-time-intended

brother-in-law is of lupine persuasion?" Timothy asks, as he walks to the shed door and pushes it partially shut. Though Matty's growls are becoming less and less loud and, thereby, less and less likely to reach anyone in the house, Timothy doesn't want to take the chance that Matty's parents might come running. If their son can so easily turn into a werewolf, the parents might still be able to manage something by way of attempted rescue.

"I certainly didn't have a clue," Melissa confesses. "Nor do I know of anyone else who ever did, either."

Matty stops struggling. His wolfish facial features melt back to human, his body quickly following suit. He's now a recognizable teenager, breathing hard, encased in the dead-weight metal jacket the bike has become.

"Sorry," he says. "It's just that when you told me about Trish..."

He's crying, though whether because his attack was foiled, or because his girlfriend and soon-to-have-been-official fiancée is dead, Timothy isn't so sure.

"I loved her so...so...so much!" Matty manages between sobs.

"Look, man," Timothy says, "no one is sorrier that Trish died than her sister and I. We just came to tell you, because we didn't want you hearing it from people who didn't care as much as we do."

"I'm so torn up inside," Matty apologizes. "I was suddenly angry at the whole world, you two included. Besides, it's not as if I'm in control of this werewolf thing, these days. It seems to be taking on an increasing life of its own."

"Admittedly, strange things are happening," Melissa is the first to agree.

"Amen," Timothy seconds, still marveling at the former bike turned modern-art sculpture caging Matty's upper body.

"Please tell me that you can get this thing off me as easily as you cocooned me in it," Matty says contritely.

"What do you think, Melissa?" Frankly, unsure how he got Matty into the full metal jacket, Timothy is even more unsure how to disrobe him of it.

"I think..." Melissa starts to say but stops.

"What?" Timothy asks. He can tell just by the expression on her face that something isn't right.

"I have to go," she says. "There's something important I have to do. You decide as to when and how to let Matty go. Or, maybe, just leave him as is," she distantly adds as she heads for the shed door.

"Go where?" Timothy is genuinely confused.

"To find a blue candle," Melissa says cryptically.

"I promise I'll fill you in later."

At which point, she's out the door and running, leaving Timothy to decided about Matty.

"What do I do with you?" Timothy wonders aloud. He's tempted to leave Matty as-is and follow Melissa. She's up to something, and he'd really like to know more about exactly what it is. Besides, in these strange times, she might need him, and he doesn't like being left out of her loop.

#70 THEN, THERE BE DRAGON?

The candle, half-burnt, continues flaming bright and steady, projecting the stream of constantly emanating images within to hover, kaleidoscope-like, in a glowing crown above the flame.

Kevin-the-momentary-dragon-now-boy-again humbly apologizes for almost burning the house down. His father's long anticipation of just such an event assured that several fire extinguishers were readily at hand throughout the house, and that the blaze was able to be quickly to put out.

"Still the doubter?" Qwan Chou asks his son, already knowing the answer.

"Kind of hard to doubt when I felt my mouth open

242

and breathe fire," Kevin admits.

"You were thinking, were you not, that being a dragon wouldn't be all that bad? You were singling out individuals you could pay back for past wrongs?"

"How did you know that?"

"It's the same way of thinking that had many of our ancestors choose to remain dragons to the bitter end. It's the kind of reasoning that may make it already too late for you to get out of here to safety. It's genuinely impossible to save someone who doesn't want to be saved."

"Would I be a dragon 24/7?"

"You would, for as long as you remain within the boundaries of this power grid, yes."

"Do you know the boundaries as they exist, here, around Flicker?"

"Only that San Francisco would certainly have you safely out of harm. The only dragons there are cloth and paper."

"I would convert back to human, though, even once a dragon, if I just passed over any one of the boundaries?"

"It will become harder and harder for you to will yourself to do that once you have become dragon and remain so for awhile," his father says. He can already see in Kevin's almost reptilian eyes the desire to possess and exercise the full power of dragon. He doesn't know whether to be happy or to be sad. It's his son's choice to make, after all, and this particular power source seems entirely disposed toward meting out transformative powers only to the teen members of the Chou family. While Qwan has purposely steered clear of rumored power areas in the past, he has been truly awed and made more than a little jealous by his son's impressively fiery performance, here, today.

"How much time do I have to decide?"

"My guess would be not long. Your fire-breathing moment saw you not completely morphed to dragon but not far from it. Certainly, you are farther along in the transformation process than I ever imagined possible. This area is possessed of more power than any other of which I've ever heard. Whether that bodes good or ill for you, and others, I can't tell."

Kevin is thinking that to be at the top of the food chain is something to definitely be desired by one, such as himself, who has never been there before. On the other hand, he wonders how many girl dragons, if any, presently occupy this same area, and if he can count upon enjoining with one at any time in the future.

"Whether or not you ever mate, you're not going anywhere for now," whispers the deep and dark voice of the dragon already rooted firmly inside his head.

#71 ANYTHING THAT CAN, WILL...

Colonel Growlan walks into Lt. Col. Loo's office, unannounced. Madison is taken aback and immediately comes to his feet.

"At ease! At ease!" Col. Growlan waves a hand as if he really doesn't mean to cause so much fuss. "I just thought I'd stop by to get a face-to-face update."

"The official search party for the photographer, Peter McGee, is formed and ready to move on your order," Madison says. "One-hundred-ten volunteers, four bloodhounds, and a helicopter. Our hope is, of course, that we're fully cognizant of everything that's transpired off-base-to-on-base, thus far. Likewise, we can only hope no member of the search party meets up with another of the things that killed McGee, or with whatever killed the thing that killed McGee."

"Amen!" Col. Growlan looks for a chair, knowing, as he does, there isn't one, other than the lieutenant colonel's. There is never spare seating in the colonel's office, either. Airmen are supposed to stand at attention, state their business, and leave again, not sit around and shoot the bull.

"A preliminary test has come back on the water, but nothing out of the ordinary has shown up, yet." Madison is still standing because his superior officer is still standing. "This doesn't mean that something won't turn up when the completed final reports come trickling in; we still have people drawing water from various other spots around the countryside and in the town."

"Our excuse?"

"Routine testing for jet-fuel contamination. The annually conducted test for that was scheduled to begin next month, anyway."

However benign the initial results, Madison is glad he called his wife and his son with instructions that they drink nothing but imported, bottled water. He promised them a detailed explanation, later, which he's going to have to make up.

"The autopsy of the creature is in progress as we speak," Madison continues. "So far, the universal consensus is that, despite its appearance, it definitely isn't a taxidermy hoax. Common name unknown, Kingdom Animalia, Phylum Chordata, Class Mammalia, and Order Carnivora—Family, Genus, species still indeterminate at this time."

The phone rings, and is answered by Lieutenant Wexlan in the outside office.

"And the thing that killed the thing that killed McGee, based upon the throat wound?" Colonel Growlan asks Madison.

"No one has a clue. First guess was a wolf, but it

would have had to be an exceptionally large one.
They've taken what they believe are saliva samples
from the wound and have shipped them to a secure
laboratory back East for detailed analysis. They've also
done castings of the teeth marks. Summary results are
not expected for awhile yet."

"Excuse me, sir," Lieutenant Wexlan interrupts,
sticking his head in from the other room, "I think you
might want to take this call."

"I think not!" Madison barks, perturbed by the
lieutenant who obviously has to learn that a visiting
colonel takes precedence over all other affairs, unless
it's a general or the President of the United States on
the other end of the line, of course.

"With all due respect, sir, it seems there's already
a rescue effort in progress in the scrublands," the
lieutenant persists, "involving someone who was
supposedly out there all night, maybe even with his
grandson in attendance."

"Just what we need," Madison says, meaning just
the opposite. As he picks up the receiver, a suddenly
very-concerned colonel, not feeling in the least bit
slighted, walks silently out.

#72 THE CANDLE PURPLE

The wick of the admittedly pathetic-looking purple candle, which Uxana with difficulty manages to refashion from the damaged conglomerate of her Sisterhood's salvaged wax, sputters and dies. More than two-thirds of its original swayed-back column, however, remains, unburnt. It puffs a sickly spiral of thin, wispy smoke toward the cave ceiling and looks no more capable of performing a second miracle than its original did of performing the first.

The experience has Uxana drained to her core, exhausted, gasping, and feeling as if all but a tiny bit of her life-force has siphoned away.

On the other hand, she's amazed that all of her efforts, as puny and lacking in every regard as they may have seemed at the time, have been well worth her while.

She's now convinced that she has retained all of the necessary instructions Zila telepathed to her before her Sister in the Sisterhood's suicide. She has carried out and performed at least one of the two required rituals correctly. She has summoned a replay of the sequence of events which culminated with a select group of ancient priestesses having boxed the Book of Answers before the last great flood to secret it in a spot that is now part of her memory. She recognizes the terrain of that hiding spot. Uxana knows how far away it is from where she now is. If she wonders how she'll possibly muster the strength and resolution necessary to get to the book to reclaim it, she's confident now that a way will somehow present itself. She has constantly doubted her ability to get this far, and all of her doubts have been thrown back in her face. Where there is a will, there is a way.

She must yet, however, somehow locate and dip into that will, despite her inclination to lie back and die. She must fight against the despair of knowing that no matter how far she has thus far come, there is yet much more to overcome, alone, with no one or thing likely to provide any assistance, except, possibly, the remaining bit of purple wax sagging all the more since having once been lit.

Perhaps what she needs is a short rest, a nap, a brief doze, just for a few minutes. She is, after all, so terribly tired. After a sleepless night and additional strength-sapping during her summoning of the vision, surely the powers that be wouldn't begrudge her a moment or two in which to regroup and...

The candle wick spontaneously re-lights in complete defiance of her desire and keeps burning until she, unconsciously, reaches forward and tries to suffocate the flickering flame to a premature death between a thumb and index finger.

"Ouch!" Her fingers are burned. The flame is not extinguishable. "Please, I just need a moment!"

"... a moment...moment...moment," her voice echoes. That, though, is all she's given in response to her plea.

Though acquiescing, she genuinely doubts she'll survive. How all-knowing can the power of the candle be, if it can't see that she is already at the end of her rope?

The flame dims, giving her hope that it is suddenly sympathetic to her needs.

All light fades except for a mere flicker that dances the center of the melting candle top.

Then, the light expands, and Uxana groans her ultimate frustration, even as it dawns on her that she and her candle are no longer in the cave that has for so long housed them.

They're in a room, at a table. Directly across from them are another girl and another candle.

Uxana has seen the girl before.

Obviously, the girl not only knows Uxana but is expecting her.

"I thought you would never come," Melissa says.

"I am here, now, though," Uxana says, "that the

two of us might be together always."

#73 ONE PLUS ONE IS ONE

"Do come in, Timothy," Mary Remoth says as she ushers the boy on through. Timothy is such a fine-looking young man, and so much more confident these days with his father dead and gone. Mary hadn't known Gyle Gril all that well, but she never much liked what little she'd heard or seen. "I've been looking for an excuse to see what Melissa has been up to, since she insisted I un-crate her aunt's birthday-gift candle."

"Melissa is candle-reading, then, is she?"

"Not only that, it had to be a blue candle." Mary shakes her head. "She was quite insistent and genuinely distraught when I told her I didn't think I had one. Luckily, I remembered the one I was supposed to send off before everything became so distracting. Melissa's Aunt Joan will have to wait until I can whip her up another."

She motions Timothy toward the chair adjoining the one in which Roger Remoth is seated.

"Look who's here, Roger."

"Timothy," Roger says distantly and nods. He's been watching yet not watching the television news for some time. He and Mary have mainly just been sitting and thinking about Trish and how she's no longer with them. "How did Matty take hearing that Trish is..." He can't yet even say the word, let alone believe that his older daughter is truly...dead.

"Not very well, I'm afraid," Timothy says. Which is neither more nor less than Melissa told them. Certainly, Timothy doesn't comment upon Matty's transformation into a werewolf, or Matty being tied down by a twisted bicycle chassis, or Matty begging long and loud to let him free, or Matty having to wait even longer for Timothy to figure out how to get everything untwisted back into its original shape.

"On second thought, Timothy, maybe you should go see what Melissa is up to," Mary decides. "Would you mind?"

"Of course not." Timothy gets up from the seat he's just taken and follows the direction of Mrs. Remoth's outstretched arm, pinpointing the closed door to the basement which the Remoth family reserves for conducting their most important candle-reads.

"Knock, but if she doesn't answer just go on in," Mary says. It's easier for her to ask someone else to intrude on Melissa than for her to do so. "Sometimes, she concentrates so hard that the whole rest of the world gets excluded."

"Right."

Melissa doesn't answer Timothy's first, second, or third knock.

He opens the door and goes downstairs.

She's sitting, calm as you please, at a table, a tall, blue candle burning in front of her. She's looking even more exceptionally pretty than usual, albeit with an unusually serious expression.

"Yes," she says. "Yes, yes. I understand."

Initially, he thinks she's talking to him but soon decides she's carrying on a one-sided conversation with the candle, or with its flame, or with the table or... The whole ambiance is spooky enough to cause chills down his backbone and tease the fine hairs up along the nape of his neck.

"Melissa?"

She stops talking but remains focused on the candle, or its flame, or the table, or....

"Melissa?" he repeats.

She leans forward over the table and blows out the candle flame. Turning to Timothy, she smiles. There's something different about her that he can't quite isolate. Not different—bad. Strange. In a bad sort of way.

"Melissa, you okay?"

"I'm fine, Timothy. Did you finally get Matty all untangled?"

"What a story that is to tell," Timothy says and would say more except Mrs. Remoth joins them.

"However did you manage to make that happen, Melissa?" Mary asks, heading for the table, and picking up the still-smoking candle. "You've managed to make this all-blue candle somehow bleed purple."

Mrs. Remoth insists that Melissa insisted the candle had to be blue. This one definitely is blue, but, as noted by an incredulous Mary, has deep purple veins all over and inside it.

"I have to go to Dry Wash Gulch," Melissa states, changing the subject. "Can you and dad drive me there now?"

"Right now?" Mary asks, fascinated by the candle in hand and wondering how to duplicate the effect. She bets there are a lot of potential customers who would be interested in purchasing one, if for no other reason than just because such a candle is so decorative.

"The sooner the better," Melissa says.

"Well, you'll have to wait until at least tomorrow afternoon, honey," Roger says, appearing suddenly at the doorway to join everyone else. "There's a search going on over there. They're looking for some missing photographer. I suspect the people in charge, if we come with our own agenda, would feel that we're getting in their way."

"How about tomorrow morning, then?"

"Trish's funeral is tomorrow morning, honey," Mrs. Remoth says softly. "Your dad and I want it to be a small and private family affair."

"Surely, Matty can come?" Melissa asks anxiously. God only knows what would happen if he wasn't invited. Maybe, he'd turn up all werewolf and start howling and drooling at the grave site, maybe even take huge bites out of the people who'd not provided him an invite.

"I've already called his mother," Mary says. "He'll be here tomorrow morning, and we'll all drive out to the cemetery, together. You're welcome to come along, too, if you'd like, Timothy."

"Thank you, Mrs. Remoth." Timothy, like Melissa, is wondering how Matty will handle his girlfriend's ultimate slide into and under the hard, cold ground.

#74 ALL THE NEWS TODAY, OH BOY!

Gregory chows down a big bowl of *Count Chocula* cereal, even though Sydney has warned him that the box was originally bought from a specialty grocer as a joke and has been sitting in the cupboard for literally years. Everyone still expects Gregory to be sick every time he goes another day substituting regular food—at the moment stale cereal and milk—for fresh blood.

Sydney is tying Timothy's tie. Timothy is about to go to Trish's funeral, leaving Roman feeling sorry that it's to be a private family affair. "I would have loved to see how Briana play-acts grieving."

Roman is at the table, flipping through the pages of the morning newspaper. Although the television is on, no one is really interested in the network morning talk show's guest, some nerdy jerk with spiked hair and glasses attempting to explain about how to deep-fry a turkey, whole.

"Hey, something from your boyfriend's old man, Sydney!" Roman announces, pinpointing at the spot in the newspaper article with the tip of his index finger.

The Public Affairs Officer at Rockpoint Air Force Base today issued an official statement expressing deep regret for the suffering obviously undergone by Mr. Jimmy-Who-Knows, but denies any Air Force maneuvers or war games occurring on the night in question. "I have no doubt but that Mr. Who Knows may have heard something," said Lt. Col. Loo…

"Hey, the stupid reporter left off the 'r' and Cooper's dad comes off as some kind of rank British toilet," Roman says.

"…perhaps the result of inner-ear trauma
related to all of the bee stings he suffered,
but we had neither men nor helicopters in
the area on that particular evening…"

"Is that what your boyfriend is telling you, these days?" Roman asks.

"He's telling me that his dad hasn't been home lately, so hasn't said much of anything within Cooper's hearing," Sydney replies.

"But Cooper divines it's something hinky, involving the military, right?"

"Cooper says you never know with the Air Force, because they're always so gung-ho about secrecy that an Air Force general will likely deny taking a dump even while he's being seen sitting on the toilet taking one."

"Certainly," Lt. Col. Toilet…

"I substituted 'Toilet' for 'Loo', in case you're wondering," Roman informs.

"I would have never guessed," Sydney says sarcastically.

...went on to say, "the Air Force, also, was not involved in any initial search of the area to find the missing photographer, identified as a Mr. Peter McGee. At that time, we were not even aware that Mr. McGee was missing..."

"Hey," Timothy says, "there's breaking news about the missing McGee guy on TV right now."

His tie-tying finished to Timothy and his satisfaction, Sydney reaches for the television volume control and turns up the sound.

...the cave filled with a cache of candles, some of which may have been burned as recently as last night, leading experts to conjecture that devil worshippers may well have been involved in the disappearance...

"Okay, then," Lt. Col. Loo says, in the Air Force base Administration Building where Col. Growlan, Mr.

Smith, and he have all just watched the same announcement, "it seems as if I need to now add Satan-worshippers to the ever-growing list of people present in a supposedly vacant scrubland, from which we removed a dead photographer and a likely mutated-by-us creature who killed him?"

#75 DON'T COME BACK, LITTLE SHEBA!

Briana's day has been absolutely *horrible!* She's so sick of Georgiana and Tania's moaning and groaning that she finally yells, "Enough is enough!" The way they carry on and on and on, anyone would think they, with Briana, intentionally meant to kill Trish Remoth. That hadn't been the case at all, no matter what new boy, Mr. Voodoo Man, Duoto Bata (ancestors from Haiti, not from Africa), was insinuating at the hospital. A sore neck had been the only thing on the agenda for Trish, merely to get her out of the cheerleading squad and insert Georgiana into her place. That it had all gone wrong, like the cat still caught on the closet wall, had to do with power dynamics suddenly all gone screwy around Flicker. Too much power was being conjured by too little magic. At least, that was Briana's take on it, from her perspective as the conjurer. As far as her father's magic, that is pretty much altogether removed from the playing board.

She rolls in her bed, trying to get comfortable.

She's thankful that Trish's funeral is a private family affair. She can only imagine what would have happened if Georgiana and Tania had been forced to stand graveside with Briana and Trish's fellow students from Flicker High. She could imagine the guilty caterwauling that would have eventually come of that!

It would be very nice if Briana could be clued in as to what is going on. Instead of helpful revelations, though, in her sleep all she gets are bizarre, broken-record-like dreams—nightmares, really—of Little Sheba.

The only thing "little" about this first of Briana's familiar spirits had been when her father brought it home as a puppy. Even then, Briana remembered being afraid of the darn dog. When it started to grow fast, outpacing Briana at a rate of about ten to one, she really took a dislike to the bitch—and vice versa.

"Sheba will be your kindred spirit," Briana's father had insisted, each and every time his daughter had insisted he get rid of the dog before dog or girl ended up dead.

As it had turned out, it was Little Sheba who kicked the bucket first, with more than a little help from

Briana who was already experimenting with spells well beyond her grade level even as a small tot.

Briana is convinced that some witches, herself included, are loners and don't need four-legged, or feathery, or scaly helpmates. Additional proof of that is how her latest, supposed feline servant has ended up trapped half in, half out of the closet wall, when all Briana had meant to do was to keep it from that continual fingernail-on-the-blackboard screeching it was always making.

She rolls again, more restless. She tries to think of a spell that'll bring on restful slumber. She knows such a spell exists and wonders why she can't remember it. Maybe, though, it's a good thing she doesn't recall it. The way things are going, it would likely put her to sleep permanently.

The bedsprings creak from some weight other than Briana's restless tossing and turning, exactly the way it felt whenever Little Sheba decided to jump on to sniff so heartily as to suck, quite literally, the air right out of Briana's body.

In fact, when Briana opens her eyes and sits up, she's quite prepared to find Little Sheba right there on the bed with her. What greets her is certainly something she can be, and has been, accused of killing, but it isn't a resurrection of her poor long-dead dog.

Frantically, Briana screams long and loud for her father.

#76 SEEING ISN'T BELIEVING

What was that white chick thinking, calling him in the middle of the night and demanding he come running? A black boy roaming around outside her house at three o'clock in the morning. Pshew! If that wasn't a prize-winning recipe for the cops to put his sorry butt in jail, there never was one. She's just lucky—to get her to shut up and to hang up—that he agreed to stop by in the full light of the morning before going to school.

No way, though, is he going to the side door as instructed. Those days are over for blacks. He's right up front just like it's his right to be. *It is his right,* he swears beneath his breath. He doesn't care about the lame excuse she gave about the side door being the private entrance to her basement "apartment." The last thing he wants is for anyone spotting him going in and out of some white female's private apartment. Briana is obviously minus more than a couple cups of vital gray matter.

"Ahhhh, you must be Mr. Voodoo Man," greets Mr. James from the open front door. "I do believe that my daughter is expecting you." He steps out on the front porch and leans around it to point to the door at the side of house. "You'll find her down there, mad as a wet hen. A very good job, by the way, young man. Briana deserves an occasional comeuppance that I'm unable to provide as of late."

"Sorry about your powers heading south, Mr. James," Duoto says casually.

"Oh, well, I had a good run while it lasted." Actually, he's far sorrier than Duoto that his powers have gone. What's more, he's feeling more and more jealous, each and every passing day, of his incompetent daughter's increasing magic. "It does seem as if you and my daughter are gathering up far more than what I'm losing. Do try to exercise a bit of moderation, what do you say?"

Duoto really doesn't know what to say. He's still at a loss for words when Mr. James gives him a reassuring pat on the back and returns into the house, shutting the door between them.

So, maybe Duoto *will* opt for the side door after all—just this once.

Briana has the door open and is standing in it even before he gets there.

"About time!" she berates, not coming off in the least appreciative that he's gone a good deal out of his way to make this pit stop for whatever cockamamie reason she may have manufactured. Hey, maybe she's just sweet on him? He's not, after all, unattractive, now, is he?

"Let's make this quick, shall we?" he says. "I have things to do and people to see."

"The quicker the better," she agrees. "Over here."

He follows her in and over to what he assumes is the door to another room. It turns out to be the door to her closet...which she jerks open.

"Out!" she commands. For a moment, Duoto thinks she means him. He soon enough realizes, though, that who she really means is...

"Holy Moly!" He takes a step back.

"You desire something, Mistress James?" Trish Remoth asks, standing there, calm and cool as you please, no indication whatsoever of having been buried in the cemetery just the day before.

#77 RAINING CATS AND...

"Mr. Voodoo Man here, having magically made you, is here to collect you, Trish, my dear," Briana says.

"What are you talking about?" Duoto asks. "I didn't have anything to do with this. Besides, wasn't it

the 'witch'—I repeat witch—of Endor in the BIBLE
who brought back the prophet Samuel for King Saul of
Israel?"

"She brought back Samuel's ghost," Briana
reminds him. "What we have here, as you can very well
see, is a bit more than Trish's ghost. Looking and
sounding very suspiciously, and, correct me if I'm
wrong, very voodoo zombie-like."

"Don't get resurrection and re-vivification
confused, missy!" Duoto insists. "The first, what we
have here, is really a highly advanced stage of Magic.
The second, which we do not have here, is simply the
effect of simple science."

"What simple science?"

"Well, maybe it's more complex than simple."

"Do you voodoo practitioners, or do you not,
bring people back from the dead as zombies?"

"Zombies haven't ever really been dead," Duoto
says. "They've merely made to look that way by use of
a distillation of a powerful narcotic obtained from the
puffer fish. All body functions are slowed down to look
death-like. Zombies aren't dead people resurrected, but
merely look-like-they're-dead people revived one little
bit at a time. I heard it from good authority that Trish,
here, succumbed of a broken neck, brought on by your
witchy spells. There isn't any come-back, like this,

available in any voodoo shop I've ever come across."

"What reason could I ever have for bringing her back, if, as you suggest, I'm the one responsible for her murder?"

"I don't know. Regret?" Duoto suggests. "Fear you'd be found out?"

"None of the above," Briana insists. "I had absolutely nothing to do with this. That leaves the list of potentially guilty parties still at just one—namely you."

"What about her boyfriend?"

"Matty? Get serious! Besides if he could bring her back, which I very well doubt, do you think he'd march her on over here to wait on me? He'd keep her to himself. So, Mr. Voodoo Man, we're right back to you, once again, aren't we?"

"And why would I bother?"

"To get back at me for denying your cleverness in having figured out how she died in the first place."

"That means you're no longer pretending her cause of death wasn't the result of you and your witchy friends sitting around a boiling cauldron and casting spells?"

"I still can't imagine how a simple formula to cause a stiff neck could somehow morph into the snapping of a vertebra."

266

"Even so, you can't deny that there are some strange things going on around here, lately, like the increase of some people's powers at the expense of others."

"Are you going to take Trish away, or am I going to have to...? Now what's that silly-assed expression on your face mean?"

"It means, I'm wondering what else you have hidden in that closet," Duoto half-asks, half-states. He strains his neck to see around Trish to where what he's sure is...

Suddenly, a large, black ball of fur launches from the closet's shadowy darkness to land smack dab on the top of Briana's head. From the four large cat paws exude long, sharp cat claws that sink in to take hold, tightly vising Briana's skull.

Simultaneously, Briana, Duoto, and Trish scream for Briana's father.

#78 FINALLY, A PURR-FECT MATCH

It isn't Briana's father, shot-gun in hand, who tames the savage beast. He and his gun-at-the-ready arrive after Trish says, "Here, Puss," and the cat performs another impressive acrobatic feat; this one leaves Briana's hair looking like a bloody bomb site and puts the wide-eyed feline safely in Trish's cradling arms.

"That wretched animal attacked me!" Briana accuses. Her arm extends, her finger points, her arm, finger, and whole body tremble uncontrollably. "Take it out back, please, father, and blow its fur-ball head off!"

"Puss told me how you locked half of her body in your closet wall," Trish says.

"Briana?" her father asks. "Is that where Puss has been all this time? Just how long has she been locked up in there, like that, with you knowing?"

"Are you telling me there was anything either of us could have done about it?" Briana asks defensively. Even though it definitely was an accident which had imprisoned the cat, Briana has immensely enjoyed the whole time the obnoxious feline hasn't been in closer attendance. "How in the heck did she get free, anyway?"

"Trish just wished me free," Puss says, "and it happened."

"And since when did you start talking?" Briana asks; Duoto's jaw has dropped so far, it's an effort for him to get his mouth closed.

"Since I found someone worth talking to," Puss says.

"Fine. Then, you're hers, and she's yours. Now, both of you feel free to leave at any time."

"We'll be staying for awhile longer, thank you for asking," Puss says, "and I wouldn't try to stop us, if I were you. I'm not an old cat, after all, and everything young around here seems to be rapidly gaining in power. You just may find that between Trish and me, you'll not be locking either of us up, or anyone else for that matter, any time soon."

"If you kids-having-fun will excuse me, then," Mr. James says, "this adult has to go to the bathroom."

#79 FOUR'S A CROWD...OR NOT?

The candle-flame, with still a third of its length to go, blazes in a burst of renewed glory, making room inside its enlarged flicker for a panoply of additional images.

The sheriff's car pulls into the trail-head parking area shortly after Mr. Remoth parks the family vehicle there. The deputy is out of his car and standing next to Mr. Remoth's auto before anyone there can even get out.

Roger rolls down his window on the driver's side.

"Mr. Remoth," Deputy Jeb Pandley greets. He's

patrolled this section of highway for nigh on two years and has had more than one friendly meet up with the Remoths before now. "Out for a bit more geology?"

"Deputy Pandley," Roger acknowledges. He's confident the two are on good terms. "I promised a colleague that I'd round him up a couple prime specimens of local obsidian from Dry Wash Gulch. I thought I'd let my daughter and her boyfriend come along for the ride and some exercise."

"Shouldn't they be in school? I heard the building inspector gave the all-clear this morning?"

"Well, what with my older daughter having just died, I figured letting these two have another day off wouldn't likely hurt them, or anyone else for that matter."

"I'm sorry as heck to hear about Trish, Mr. Remoth," says Jeb, successfully detoured. "Terrible shame!"

Melissa and Timothy provide their very best we-really-aren't-truants expressions.

"You do know, though, that the area around here may not be nearly as safe as it once was?" Jeb says by way of follow-up.

"I know that a good many people are looking for that missing photographer but haven't found him, yet," Roger says. "I know they found some cave, filled with ceremonial candles of supposedly satanic origins. All of the activity, you'd think, will have driven away anyone who might have had any real further inclination for mischief, wouldn't you agree? Besides, I'll be in and out well before nightfall."

Jeb considers. He doesn't have any real authority to keep anyone out, only to warn them of possible consequences—whatever they might be. Not that the Remoths haven't been coming here for ages, even before the recent rash of strange deaths and mutilations of animals, wild and domestic, that have, since, become part of the area's emerging suburban legend. This missing photographer and candle-cave business, not to mention the dead Remoth girl's kidnapping, are just more weirdnesses to add to a long, and getting-longer-by-the day, list.

"Tell you what," Jeb decides. "If I can get permission from the office, what say I hike on in with you, just to make sure you're safe and sound? It would surely put my mind a whole lot more at ease. I can use the exercise, and it's a slow day. Nor is where you're headed all that far."

"I really don't think that necessary, Deputy Pandley. In fact..."

"Just let me go radio in and check," Jeb interrupts, paying Roger's protest no mind as he does a smart and briskly executed military right face and heads back to his patrol car.

"And if he gets permission to join us?" Timothy asks.

"We work around him, pure and simple," Melissa says. "Dad or you will merely provide him with some sort of diversion to keep him occupied for the few minutes it will take me to find and get what we've come for. Despite all of the information it supposedly holds, it's a comparably small book. Or, so my...instincts...tell me."

"You really think it's just going to take a few minutes to find?" Roger asks. "We've been here before —done this before—got the t-shirt or, rather, not got the t-shirt before."

"I know far more about what I'm doing this time," Melissa assures him.

"And you have somehow been thoroughly enlightened by having read that very blue candle that ended up mysteriously bleeding purple?"

"Yes."

"Well, then, if you're not concerned that the deputy will get in the way, why should I be?"

"Let's go," Jeb says, returning with an enthusiastic grin. "I haven't hiked Dry Wash Gulch for some time."

#80 IT'S A BIRD. IT'S A PLANE. IT'S...IT'S...

It's only fitting that, when Cooper sees "it" high above in the night sky, a momentary shift in the soft evening breeze wafts in his direction a puff of acrid smoke from the briquettes burning in the outside barbecue. His watering eyes blur the image which disappears into nothingness.

A moment later, Lt. Col. Madison Loo emerges from the back of the house, holding the necks of two bottles of Coke in one hand.

"Drink up!" Madison hands his son a bottle and takes the lawn chair kitty-corner from the hammock in which Cooper is lounging.

"I suggest you do the same," Cooper says. "You'll not likely finish more than a couple of swallows before you get the call to return to the air base." As for the three steaks, the potatoes and corn cobs wrapped in aluminum foil, all on the platter adjacent to the fire pit, waiting for the flames to fade to coals fit for cooking, at least one serving of each will be left uneaten. "You're the one to whom everyone will turn to explain away the dragon."

"Dragon?" Madison's cell phone rings. He answers it.

"The dragon," Cooper repeats with a sigh. If it's

not one thing, it's another. The brouhaha regarding the missing photographer finally tapers off and now . . .

"Are you sure some jet in the area didn't report an engine flare out?" Madison asks whoever is on the other end of the line.

"It's not a jet engine flare-out, dad," Cooper says as much to himself as to his father.

"I'll be there as soon as I can," Madison says, shutting the lid of his phone and slipping it back into his pocket. He focuses his full attention on his son. "A dragon?"

"Sure looked like one to me," Cooper says. "It flew over just a few minutes ago. Flames were coming out its mouth, not its rear, by the way. So unless the plane in question was flying backwards . . ."

"You and I know that there are no such things as dragons."

"You and I do know, though, that Mr. McGee, out photographing in the scablands, was attacked and partially eaten by something mighty strange and mighty big, who was chewed upon in kind, don't we?"

"I may know that," Madison says very, very slowly and very, very carefully. "Other authorized military personnel may know that, but do you really know that, son?"

"Tell me, Lt. Col. Loo," Cooper says in his best

imitation of a media correspondent, "were the eaten parts of Mr. McGee's body dragon-cooked before they were consumed?"

"You're talking more of those intuitions of yours, aren't you, Cooper," Madison says. It isn't a question, and it doesn't sound as if his statement refers to anything good, either. "I can only repeat the same conversation you and I have had several times before. Keep what you intuit to yourself or tell only me. Do not under any circumstances repeat them to anyone else. If you do, those you tell will either think I've been talking out of turn, or will take your premonitions seriously and lock you away as a laboratory specimen likely off-limits to even your mother and me. Either way, that wouldn't bode well for our family."

Mrs. Loo sticks her head out the backdoor. "Honey! Colonel Growlan's on the land line. He says it's urgent."

Madison gets to his feet.

"By the way, dad, are we still supposed to keep drinking bottled water even though all your experts continue to report the local water supply isn't tainted?"

"Yes, please." Madison heads for the house.

"It isn't the water that's causing all the weirdness, dad!" Cooper calls after him.

#81 WHEN IS A TEEPEE NOT A TEEPEE?

"Long time no see," Melissa says to Johnny-Three-Spirits who answers the front door.

"I've been staying home to take care of my grandfather, since they've let him out of the hospital." Johnny says. "Granddad still has trouble seeing."

"You know Timothy Gril?" Melissa mentions her companion standing next to her.

The two young men nod in passing acquaintance.

"Ever track down that missing video tape from the school security room?" Melissa asks, taking advantage of Johnny stepping to one side to let Timothy and her on through.

"You told Timothy about that, did you?" Johnny asks and wonders how many more people she's told.

"Timothy is now officially my boyfriend. We share most everything."

Neither Timothy nor Johnny misses her qualifying "most."

"I still haven't a clue where that tape is off to," Johnny admits. He takes a seat and lets the other two take their own. "Do you?"

"Actually, we're not here about the security tape," Melissa says. "We're here because I've had another visitation from the girl in blue."

Johnny comes to the edge of his seat. "Have you, now?"

"She led me to suspect that something of interest to all of us, by way of answers, was secured in a certain obsidian box in a certain cave in the scablands at Dry Wash Gulch."

"And?"

"And while the obsidian box is there, it's presently empty."

"Damn!"

"Leaving us to wonder if you have any clue as to what these might mean?" Melissa pulls out a piece of paper and hands it over. "They were crudely scratched on the lid of a box so expertly made that we're thinking they weren't done by the person who made the container. My father, as a geologist, can explain to you the skill required and the difficulties encountered when working with something as brittle as volcanic glass. The runes, by comparison, are quite primitive."

"An inverted capital triangle over an inverted lower-case u, next to an owl," Timothy says, as if it's Johnny-Three-Spirits, not Jimmy-Who-Knows, who's the one with impaired eyesight.

"The 'teepee,'" Melissa says, "got us to thinking some kind of Native American origin. That suddenly put you in the need-to-know loop."

"Actually, it's not a teepee," Johnny says. "If you went back and took a closer look, I think you'd see that the seeming V you've provided, here, isn't really closed at its tip, at all, but left open."

"You are familiar with it, then?"

"I've seen these scratches once before," he says. "I was five or six at the time, in the woods, and with my grandfather. They were incised on a cliff face."

"And signify what?" Melissa is excited.

"The inverted small-case u isn't that at all, but the representation of an ax head. It signifies something prepared for transit, like a tree cut down, or an animal killed. The tilted lines to either side represent the poles trailing behind a dog or horse and slung with a frame … a travois used for transporting goods and belongings.""And the owl?" Melissa and Timothy ask in unison.

"The inscriber was dealing with something deemed sacred, like a stone fallen from the sky … before, of course, it was realized meteorites are merely normal astronomical junk. Whatever the object the person in question had in hand, though, it was transported from where it was found, where the runes were left, to someplace set aside for such sacred things."

"Which around Flicker is precisely where?"

278

Melissa asks.

"On that, I haven't a clue."

Melissa and Timothy simultaneously wonder whether Johnny, dealt a winning hand by them, is now going to try and shut them out of the game.

"Really, I don't," Johnny insists, knowing exactly what they're thinking. "So few things are thought sacred any more that the locations of any such caches have long since been forgotten."

"Knowledge never to be recovered?" Melissa presses.

"Johnny!" Jimmy-Who-Knows calls from the other room. "Is there someone out there with you?"

#82 THE GOLDEN WAY, THE ONLY WAY?

"I'd better go no closer," Jimmy-Who-Knows says. He's tired. He looks tired. He's not all that long up from extended bed rest. He's only here, now, because he wants to be here, needs to be here, for his grandson, in case something goes wrong. Even in the best of times, things can go wrong, and these were definitely not the best of times.

"I suppose Timothy and I should stay back here as well," Melissa says. She and her boyfriend each wear full overalls secured tightly at sleeve ends, cuffs, and necklines. Each carries a welder's mask borrowed from Roger Remoth's workshop at home. Their uniforms aren't exactly standard beekeeper garb, but they hope they're enough protection if Johnny has to be pulled out of harm's way. Hopefully, the bees won't attack, in that they're supposed to be friendly toward local shamen. In this case, that would be Johnny, Jimmy having obviously ceded all powers to him at the whim of the powers that be.

"Okay, then," Johnny says. Unlike his peers, he wears nothing special. To do so might confuse the bees and make them wonder why, if Johnny is a real shaman, he comes to them in disguise. Needless to say, though, he's more than a little uneasy, being so vulnerably exposed. If they swarmed him once (and they had) and left him unharmed (and they had), that isn't to say they'll not sting him this time, especially since this time he's coming to take their wax and honey. "Let me give it a try."

"You sure you want to?" Jimmy asks. After what happened to him, he's genuinely fearful for his grandson's safety. After having spontaneously insinuated that the only way to provide a possible answer to the riddle of the runes inscribed on the empty obsidian box might be to query a magical scrubland-bee golden candle, he now regrets having done so. In the past, he could have likely accomplished the deed of gathering the wax and honey, himself. In these weird times though, when those who had power have it no longer, and those who had little power suddenly have too much to control, everything, including success, is less certain. Had he more strength left in him, Jimmy even now might physically try to restrain his grandson from this possible madness. As it is, the trip has almost completely sapped the remainder of Jimmy's stamina and mental acuity.

"We all need answers, don't we?" Johnny says by way of reinforcing his conviction to do what he's proposing. "If this provides us with at least the first of other answers, and if I'm the one presently best equipped to ferret out this all-important first answer, I don't think I should chicken out when there's a good chance everything will work out okay."

"Except, we've all seen the results of what can happen if things don't work out okay," Timothy says, playing Devil's Advocate. "Remember, please, that it's no sure thing that we can come to your rescue, or get you to the hospital in time, even if we free you of bees who've somehow forgotten the helpful role they're supposed to play."

"Remember, then, that pee helps," Johnny says.

"But we'll never know if this boat is going to come in, unless we—I—set it to sail."

He steps away from them. In the distance, a cloud of scrubland bees buzzes restlessly. Johnny is certain it's the same hive of bees that attacked and mauled his grandfather. The same bees that swarmed Johnny, once before, leaving him unharmed. The same kind of bees that have been the friend and helpmate of Native American shamen in these parts for eons.

In his mind's-eye, grotesque visions of his horribly bloated grandfather being stuck by thousands of sharply barbed stingers injecting their debilitating poison flash before of him.

He shivers, although he's sweating. Slowly—ever so slowly—he approaches the bees swarming before the crack in the stone.

Continuing forward, he bravely sidesteps the guard bees that protect the entrance to the hive, and peers into the bee-clogged interior of the aperture, to find the lone, vertical stack of honeycomb.

He slowly reaches in and takes hold of all that cloying stickiness, and with a firm grip gives the column a forceful tug.

#83 LOCATION, LOCATION, LOCATION

No one in the room can deny the candle created by Johnny-Three-Spirits is anything less than a visual stunner.

It dominates the center of the table.

It's a seemingly sheer column of pure light in which floats variegated honey, and chunks of honeycomb, and even the occasional scrubland bee inadvertently entombed when the materials were gathered—with scrubland bee permission—from the hive outside of Flicker. It has a prehistoric amber-like look, not yet completely solidified, within whose transparency all sorts of wondrous things can be seen, beheld, and marveled.

"It's a shame to light the wick that will put this beauty to fire," Melissa says. Nonetheless, she prepares to do just that. Mr. and Mrs. Remoth and Jimmy-Who-Knows are all sitting on the couch off to one side. No longer possessed of any real power, their participation in the ritual is merely as bystanders—witnesses to the sculpting of an entirely new world. It's the Remoth daughter and the Native American's grandson who alone currently possess sufficient power to summon an answer to the question to be asked, if, indeed, there is any answer to be found.

"Are we ready, then?" Johnny asks and provides his chair with the final inch of scoot to bring his muscled stomach firmly against the table edge.

"Do you think it will let me light the wick?" Melissa asks mystically. Quite possibly it is Uxana, now part of Melissa, who is doing the asking.

"We can see," Johnny says and puts off reaching for the candle-lighter to one side.

Melissa passes her right hand across the top of the candle, once, twice, thrice.

"Will you allow me the privilege of lighting you afire?" Melissa-Uxana asks the candle in finale.

The candle's wick bursts into spontaneous flame.

"Ohhhhhh!" Mary Remoth sighs her appreciation of the way the light from the burning candle bathes the room and everyone in it within a mystical, flickering, moving, liquid-like, golden wash. Running a hand along her arm, it's as if she can actually feel an additional layer of magical something that suddenly coats her with tangibly viscous warmth.

Johnny thinks he can taste the sweetness of scabland-bee honey on his tongue. So does Timothy, who says as much. Melissa nods her head in agreement.

The three at the table join hands.

Johnny, the candle's creator, and the shaman-benefactor of the bees who donated their honey, wax, and their lives for this moment, says a short prayer in a dialect long-forgotten and summons with great difficulty the last, fading memory of all things magical from his grandfather's mind.

There's a brief moment of silence, after which Johnny says, "We here together call upon wick and wax and honey and bees, to provide, in the flame of this golden candle, an answer to a question about an assumed sacred artifact taken from an obsidian box at Dry Wash Gulch."

The candle flame flares brightly, flickers, then decreases to normal intensity and burns calmly and steadily once again.

"Something, perhaps a book," Johnny continues, "found by one of my ancestors. Something not likely one of ours, though, but, rather, from another time, maybe even another place. Something, even if not understood, obviously sacred and of great enough importance to be transported for safe-keeping to the place where sacred things were then stored. A record of that transportation left behind in three runes carved on the top of the original glass container. Those runes are the head of an ax, the poles of a travois, and the image of an owl."

"We need to find the object in question," Johnny, Timothy and Melissa say in unison.

The beneficent golden candle, its flame wrapped in a shimmering golden aura, tells them within the flame what they want to know.

To which Timothy's spontaneously immediate response is a heartfelt, "Oh, dear!"

#84 SURVIVOR: TEAM SHADOW

He flows on the wall like rain water on a metal playground slide and pours himself into coagulated human form behind the podium.

Every one—and thing—invited is already in his, her, or its seat, waiting.

"I am back," he says, extending to either side of his shadowy corpus what looks like a translucent, grey arm draped in translucent grey cloth.

The room fills with restless murmurs.

"No need to state the obvious," someone says. Another echoes agreement. They know he's back, or they wouldn't be here. It's the information they've commissioned him to bring back that they're anxious to hear.

"Those of you who are losing powers *here*, will not regain them *there*," he says. Since his audience wants it delivered hard and fast, he obliges. "Go there, and you'll still lose them, only faster."

The ensuing murmurs, this time, are purely of disappointment. He's dosed them collectively with a bitter pill that's proving difficult to swallow.

"All the powers of young and old drain from here to there," he says. "From there, the powers flow only to the young." Then, just to be cruel, since no one in his august audience is under the age of thirty, he says, "So, if you're a teenager, go to Flicker and rejoice. Quickly enough, you'll have more magic than you have any idea how to use."

He makes the room go dark and activates the DVD machine inside the dais. The large flat television screen that separates the stage drapery behind him lights up.

"Observe, if you will, two such teenagers in Flicker," he says and waves his presenting human arm and hand in the direction of the two suddenly on show. "Pay particular note to the boy sitting at the desk in the Flicker High School hallway."

There is no accompanying audio, but it's obvious the two teenagers on the screen are engaged in a heated conversation, culminating with the hurried exit of the girl. Behind her, the boy visibly morphs from human … to snake … to cougar … to wolf ... and back to human!

A horrified gasp arises from the audience in

unison. These people and these things know unbound excess when they see it. They've spent their whole lives —some very, very long lives—managing powers that were gifted them, most of the powers having already left, or currently in the hurried process of exiting. They know a spigot vomiting magic full force when they see one, and this one in Flicker, with no one there to tighten the tap to provide moderation, is entirely out of control.

The boy is, suddenly, wolf again, scrambling for traction on the slippery hallway floor, looking ridiculous, even silly . . . nervous laughter . . . as he manages his unflattering scramble of an escape—finally —successfully—through the open door.

"Those young fools will kill themselves and us alike!" someone says. Others murmur in agreement. The volume of additional assents increases.

"Stop and think!" he commands loudly from the stage, no longer needing the microphone. He's been projecting his powerful voice for years to get attention when needed. Now, as in the past, he realizes immediate success. "What we need do is recruit our own group of teenagers to insert, along with us, into the Flicker equation. What we need do is control those unable to control themselves." It's so obvious a solution that he can't believe they haven't all already grasped the concept. "Certainly, we need to get a firm hold, before these youths gain mastery over their gifts. We, who have had in the past, but who are now losing our gifts, must move, decisively, swiftly, now, to manipulate the powers of those who have them, or will soon have them, or we will be left entirely without recourse."

"Here! Here!" come the loud, boisterous, unanimous responses of enthusiastic and total agreement.

#85 RESTRAINT VS. RESTRAIN

Once Timothy snap-decides to restrain all of them, it's easy enough to accomplish. He has become quite proficient with his skill; what with the practice on his late father and, more recently, on Matty the werewolf.

Melissa isn't surprised by his ability, she's just surprised that he's done it to her, and looks as betrayed as she feels. Timothy, on the other hand, hopes he'll be able to erase that painful expression from her face, as well as remove the bindings from her wrists and ankles in a short time.

The others are as shocked by his ability to subdue them as they are by how he has somehow so quickly summoned cords from lamps, wire hangers from the closets, sashes from the drapes, even silverware from the kitchen drawers (the knives, forks, spoons, pots and pans combining to form the welded weave that now pins Mrs. Remoth to the couch), to come flying and spinning and twisting and turning and wrapping and knotting, apparently of their own accord.

"This isn't what it looks like," Timothy tries to explain.

"Funny," Melissa says, "but it sure looks and feels as if I'm tied up."

"If it looks like a duck..." Johnny-Three-Spirits adds.

"It's only temporary, until I can explain. I don't want you all going all hyper on me."

"Something to do with the Book of Answers being cached in a spot directly beneath Briana James' house?" Melissa asks.

"Something to do with that, yes," Timothy admits, "but something other than that, too. More to do with what else we're going to find in the basement."

"Which you've determined we shouldn't do," Johnny says; it's not a question.

"Oh, no! Of course, we should do it," Timothy surprises. "It's just that I have something I need to reveal, particularly to Mr. and Mrs. Remoth, and

Melissa, here, before we show up on Briana's doorstep with shovels and picks and..."

"A jackhammer. I suggest a jackhammer. They have so many uses..." Mr. Remoth injects into the pregnant pause; construction and destruction are subjects he knows very well, while what Timothy has done—trussing Roger up like a stuck pig—is something about which the man hasn't a clue, especially now that all of his magic has deserted him.

"Something, I'm afraid, I need to let Matty Donnelly know, too," Timothy decides. In for a dime, in for a dollar.

"After first restraining him?" Melissa asks facetiously.

"By all means, yes," Timothy agrees, "knowing what we know about his volatility and how easily he can shift to werewolf in the mere blink of an eye, daylight or night."

"So, Matty Donnelly is a werewolf, just as I suspected!" Jimmy-Who-Knows says with smug satisfaction. "I wasn't hallucinating in that cave, after all."

"Yes, but what I need to tell you has to do with Trish," Timothy says, getting the shocked expressions expected all along, and he's not even told them what he needs to reveal to them about her yet.

"What about Trish?" Mr. and Mrs. Remoth immediately want to know.

"Roman Michaels..." Timothy pauses. Really, he wishes he knew how this was going to play out. Certainly, he doesn't like the possibilities it has for ruining his relationship with Melissa. She's his first girlfriend, and he really enjoys the way things have been going between them. It's really been the prospect of spoiling what he has with her that has kept him holding onto his secret so long.

"What about Roman Michaels and Trish?" Johnny eggs him on.

"Roman has...at least I think he has...been persuaded by our guardian to...well..."

"By Mr. Ranlin to...well...what?" Melissa, as well as the others, is obviously not about to be denied the answer.

"Sort of bring Trish back from the dead," Timothy reluctantly confesses.

#86 OUT OF THE CLOSET

Melissa suspects it's her possession by Uxana that is presently providing her with the inner calm needed to deal with each successive, unexpected turn of events.

She only wishes Matty had things as much together as she does. That obviously not being the case, she wishes Timothy would at least do what he said he planned to do and tie Matty up instead of taking Matty at his word that he'll wait patiently in the car until the all-okay signal is given.

"I should be in there. I should be in there. I should be in there." Matty keeps repeating over and over and over, staring at the James' house, hand-pounding the car dashboard in accompaniment as if he's playing bass-drum in a rock band.

Melissa keeps expecting him to turn werewolf—as Timothy predicted he would do and as Matty initially did, when Melissa and Timothy finally told him about the sudden undead status of his girlfriend and fiancée.

At least, by comparison, Mr. and Mrs. Remoth are now more laid back. Or, more likely, in renewed shock. As if the very idea that Trish might be resurrected by one of Gregory Ranlin's wards isn't enough, the couple now faces the probability that Trish, returned to them, might not—how had Timothy put it? —oh, yes—"be quite the same as before."

Despite wanting to be there, Jimmy-Who-Knows isn't with them. The last few days have left his poor old bones dragging, and no way could he be expected to man an ax, pick, shovel, or jackhammer, for the proposed recover-the-artifact activities. He's back at his house in bed—whether sleeping or not, what with all that's going on, is anyone's guess.

Timothy opens the side door of the James' house and gives a come-hither curl with his right hand to beckon those impatiently waiting in the car outside.

Matty is out of the auto faster than a bolt of lightning. Melissa expects Timothy to launch some inanimate object to restrain, or at least slow him down, but, to her surprise and consternation, it doesn't happen.

Matty makes it all of the way to the house and barrels through the door, before mom and dad Remoth, by comparison, can exit the car.

Matty is brought up short by the sight of Briana and her father secured, Timothy-style, on the bed.

"Where's Trish?" he asks anyone and everyone in the room who may have an answer. The only one who tries to respond is Briana, whom Timothy has gagged with a rolled-up sock for fear she might commence some witchy incantation and screw up a plan that has, so far, worked pretty much perfectly.

"These two," Johnny-Three-Spirits says, joining the quickly growing crowd and motioning toward the trussed duo, "seem to think that she's hiding in the closet, over there."

"Not exactly hiding," Mr. James, relaxing in his

bonds, begs to differ. "She and Puss actually seem to like it in there. Something about 'good vibes'."

"Puss who?" Matty beats Melissa to the punch.

"Puss, the cat," Timothy says, beginning his promised explanation. Johnny and he, having already heard the story, agree to leave Trish unrevealed until Matty's arrival. "Puss, the witch Briana's familiar, who has apparently decided to move on to something better —namely, Trish—saying what about Briana when her familiar prefers the undead?"

Briana grunts an objection to his comment, struggling unsuccessfully in her bindings.

Matty goes to the closet door and tears it open.

Trish steps out, calm as you please, Puss purring in her arms.

Everyone, including Mr. James and Briana, witness Trish looking very much alive.

"Honey!" Matty proclaims, so overcome with joy that he actually starts to cry.

"Matty?" Trish asks as if not really quite sure. "Is that really you?"

"About damned time!" says Puss, exiting Trish's arms onto the floor with a heavy thud, so the two lovers can reunite in joyous embrace without squashing him between them.

#87 WHO CHECKED OUT THE BOOK OF ANSWERS?

The book recovery process is aided by Roger, since his company built all surrounding residences and he knows the floor plans by heart.

When Melissa and he calculate that digging should commence beneath the floor of the James' basement closet, no one is at all surprised, having repeatedly heard how Trish and Puss find the closet so full of good vibes.

There are, though, complications.

The neighbors have to be informed the ensuing noise is from basement remodeling and, yes, will be kept to a minimum. The inquiring secretary at Flicker High School has to be told that Briana and Timothy have come down with "something" that, should they attend school, would indubitably be passed on to all their classmates. Mr. James' and Mr. Roger's secretaries need to find out that their bosses are suffering from whatever "bug" is going around, and the men will be out of their offices for at least forty-eight hours.

In fact, it takes two full days of hard excavating to break into the small, deeply located, stone cavity that holds the cache of sacred items hidden so long ago by rune-etching early Native Americans. Wherever the natural entrance had once been, it is long since gone, sealed perhaps by ground collapse due to earthquakes or, more likely, simply from all of the construction above ground.

What ultimately surprises and disappoints is how the cache, once accessed, doesn't yield the desired object any more than did the empty obsidian box at Dry Wash Gulch.

"No Book," Timothy announces the obvious.

There are, however, several individual stones, some rough, some not, some pretty, some not; one, translucent olive green, is downright beautiful. There's a small, carved piece of pale creamy stone, or ivory, or bone, of a very fat or pregnant woman with hair piled as high as she is tall. There's a dead and wilted, possibly pressed, flower of a variety no one has ever seen before. There are numerous, scattered stone beads, of various colors, sizes, and crudeness, that might or might not have once been strung together into a bracelet or necklace whose cord has long since rotted away. There's a very small, much chipped, and decidedly plain ceramic bowl containing absolutely no indication that it ever contained anything. There's a small piece of fabric that dissolves completely at Trish's mere touch, as well as sundry other items not readily identifiable. Finally, there's the remnant of an old candle, white with contrasting lumps of inherent caramel wax, assumed used to provide light when adding or removing items from the collection.

Truth be told, the excavators' disappointment is more than offset by their pleasure in having Trish back with them and seemingly so little the worst for wear in having died and been resurrected, despite Timothy's dire predictions based on what he'd heard about the undead from within the Ranlin household.

Melissa is happy that her sister, despite everything, seems increasingly more alive and well. The Uxana part of Melissa, however, is genuinely distraught. One-hundred percent certain that the superb, golden honey-and-wax scrubland-bee candle had pointed them correctly to the Book and its expected answers, she fights at acquiescing to the thought that all she needed and sought must remain unsolved.

Timothy and Johnny, while decidedly happy for the resulting joyous family reunion, wish for all their effort they'd uncovered something more.

"I'll take these artifacts to my grandfather for safe-keeping," Johnny says. No way is he about to leave them, whether truly sacred or not, in the caretaking of witchy Briana and her once-upon-a-time-warlock father.

"There are garbage bags in the kitchen that you can use for transport." Mr. James is helpful, not wanting the things around any more than Johnny wants them left there. They give Mr. James the creeps. It's like discovering his house having been built atop an Indian burial mound. Besides which, God only knows what mischief his maligned daughter will make of the artifacts if left anywhere where she could get her spell-casting hands on them. He blames Briana entirely for this unneeded and unwanted interruption in his life, including the loss of his very-much-missed magical powers—not to mention his anger over the huge hole, the piles of dirt, and the all-around mess that now exists as a result of the basement dig-in.

#88 DON'T JUDGE A BOOK BY ITS COVER

It's the candle! Of course, it's the candle!

Melissa is embarrassed that she didn't recognize it as such from the get-go, especially in that both she and Uxana-within come from long lines of candle-readers.

Melissa, however, makes it seem a mere afterthought, asking Johnny if it would be all right if she keeps the partially-burned column of wax as a souvenir—to which he readily agrees. It seems no more logical to him than to anyone else that the weary-looking candle could ever be included within the count of sacred treasures gathered and cached by his forefathers.

Interesting that they had all—including Melissa/ Uxana—expected the Book of Answers to be a stereotypically recognizable, printed-words-on-crumbling-paper book with a cracking hardback binding.

The state of the candle was the primary clue to the contrary. As surely as other people must have, during one disaster or another, set out in search for the Book of Answers, surely a few must have succeeded. A regular book would have become soiled, pages torn, pages dog-eared, spine creased.

That the candle is partially melted, with more than two-thirds of its original molding gone, indicates not use, abuse, and distress whenever it provided incidental lighting for caretakers supplementing or temporarily removing and utilizing the treasures, but, instead, a series of successful past candle-reads.

"Do you think by reading what remains of the candle, you could possibly get some clue to the whereabouts of the Book of Answers?" Timothy surprises Melissa with his insight. His forte, while not reading candles, still surrounds manipulating inanimate objects to shift and move, twist and bend, distort and corkscrew—and this candle has been well-manipulated in the past.

"I doubt what's left of this sorry bit of wax could even reveal whomever last opened the Book," Melissa says, "let alone help anyone learn where the Book was next hidden." It's not exactly a lie.

Melissa knows deep in her heart that she should confess success to everyone present, especially to her boyfriend, but she's determined to savor the moment all to herself awhile longer. Besides, she may be wrong—though she very much doubts that she is. Also she sees it as imperative that neither Briana nor Mr. James be made privy to fact of the Book's recovery, if the Book in the form of a candle is, in fact, recovered.

"Still, I can try to read it, later," she qualifies. "Right now, I'm too tired to endure any more disappointment."

That said, the evening of that very same day, her parents and Trish asleep—the latter, it's finally been agreed, to be introduced in Flicker as Melissa's visiting "cousin" Maleena from Portland—Timothy, Johnny, Matty, Briana and Mr. James hopefully sound asleep in their beds, Melissa places the retrieved candle on the table in front of her and puts its wick to flame.

Concentrating fully on the flame, she asks the candle if it is the Book of Answers.

"Yes," it replies in a soft, wispy, and decidedly

feminine mental voice. "Be forewarned that all of the answers I give will melt away with me, so choose wisely what you ask and be quick. You may well find there are other far more important questions to ask of me at some later date."

#89 WISH WISELY, SAID THE GENIE

Melissa is disturbed by how quickly time elapses during the burn. She's disturbed by how the Book of Answers candle height has depreciated significantly since she began asking questions. She's disturbed, but also elated, to finally receive some answers, though she wishes that she could keep them all to herself, to use in her own part yet to be played in the ongoing game—and it is a game—a game of ultimate power—which she, by necessity, must share with her future allies in order to narrow, and eventually stop, the daily increasing number of game-players wanting to enter the playing field.

She knows that the area around Flicker is the center of the Earth's source of Magical Power, from the time the planet was conceived. She knows that the area's emanations have increased and decreased over millennia and that it has to do with changes induced by major astronomical and geological events—meteorite showers, volcanic eruptions, lava flows, earthquakes, landslides, tectonic plate movements, and a series of Biblical-proportion floods. Temporary lulls in the catastrophic sequences occur, the most recent allowing the power of the place to increase beyond all previous levels to the point of at last beginning to realize its sole purpose: that of causing the selection and molding of a final, lone, Grand Master Magician, sole holder of Magic—someone young and vibrant—able to oversee the development of the Earth, and everyone and everything thereon.

Melissa now knows that everyone and everything over the age of nineteen with any magical capabilities in and around Flicker is being drained of power, and that that power is being simultaneously re-routed into the teenagers presently gathered in and around the ancient flow—all recipients deemed worthy candidates for Grand Master Magician status.

She knows struggle will soon ensue, and the winner will be the teenager who gathers up the most Magic, first from elders, then peers, to finally stand triumphant. Whether a good or evil person—all definitions of good and evil being relative—is of no importance. The only thing that matters now is how the game is played and won.

For the benefit of humankind—and there are an infinite number of other "kinds" living, half-living, and non-living beings, wishing to inhabit and control the Earth—Melissa, possessed of Uxana, can't help but think of herself as the best candidate to assume the position of ultimate Magical Power. Certainly, as the events of recent days flash before her in the candle flame, as she leans forward and blows out the considerably shrunken Book of Answers flame, she's determined that someone as evil and witchy as Briana James will never know of or sit on the Grand Master Magician's throne.

#90 SURVIVOR: TEAM MELISSA / UXANA

Melissa invites Trish, Timothy, Matty, Johnny, Sydney, Roman, and Cooper into the room. With the exception of herself and Uxana, the girl in blue now flourishing within her, Melissa, the only one possessed of the most of the answers, has determined that of her friends gathered around her, only she must sit on the Grand Master Magician's throne. Certainly, she doesn't trust the last three and wouldn't have brought them into her confidence if she didn't specifically need nine teenagers to perform the incantation, the second deed, as revealed in the flame of the Book of Answers. They are necessary to exponentially increase and release Melissa's power, ultimately increasing the odds of winning the game.

She has told her allies of the moment only what they need know—about what has been, is, and will be happening all around them—to assure their cooperation.

If they rightly suspect she's not telling them everything, they nonetheless feel privileged to know what they do know, which is certainly more than is known by the myriad other players in the game. Such information will provide a distinct advantage in deciding who does and who doesn't succeed in the end.

"We're all in agreement, then, to seal off the area?" Melissa asks. She knows the answer, but it's part of the magical process that must be followed to achieve the desired result.

"We are all in agreement," they say as one.

"Then, let's join hands," she says, and, as instructed, they chant the spell: "The deed is done...the deed is done...the deed is done. The area is sealed. The seal will remain unbroken until the Grand Master Magician sits triumphant on the throne. Permanent annihilation to any and all who break the seal. *Quilbad...Quoxum...Motatium estas regulum...Tat*

Lexicum Maxumus Rex."

"Amen," the group intones in unison.

Outside sirens begin to wail.

"The Air Force has already detected the seal-in," Cooper divines.

Although pleased with the quick evidence of their success, Melissa intuits that at least some of the evil she means to prevent from entering the area has already entered and is now sealed with the rest of them inside the playing field. In verification, beneath the wailing of the sirens, the newly formed alliance hears a chorus of bone-chilling howls and screeches of the very ones they will inevitably have to face during the undetermined times ahead.

END OF BOOK 1

About the Author

William Maltese was born in the Pacific Northwest. He has a B.A. in Marketing/Advertising and spent an honorable tour of duty in the U.S. Army, achieving the rank of E-5. He started his authorial career, which has now extended over four decades, by writing for men's pulp magazines. He has penned more than 200 books, both fiction and nonfiction, including his children's book DOG ON A SURFBOARD AND THE REST OF THE ADVENTURE under the pen name Billy Lambert. His esteemed credentials have earned him, among many other accolades, a listing in the prestigious WHO'S WHO IN AMERICA. His websites include:

http://www.williammaltese.com
http://www.myspace.com/williammaltese
http://www.myspace.com/draqual
http://www.myspace.com/flickerwarriors
http://www.myspace.com/maltesecandlegallery
http://www.mxi.myvoffice.com/williammaltese

If you enjoyed *Flicker: #1-Book of Answers* consider these other fine Books from Savant Books and Publications:

Dare to Love in Oz by William Maltese

A Whale's Tale by Daniel S. Janik
Tropic of California by R. Page Kaufman
The Village Curtain by Tony Tame
The Interzone by Tatsuyuki Kobayashi
Today I Am A Man by Larry Rodness
The Bahrain Conspiracy by Bentley Gates
Called Home by Gloria Schumann
Kanaka Blues by Mike Farris
Poor Rich by Jean Blasiar
First Breath: 2010 Savant Anthology of Poems, edited by Zachary Oliver
The Jumper Chronicles by W. C. Peever

Scheduled for Release in 2010:
Mythical Voyage by Robin Ymer
Ammon's Horn by Guerrino Amati
My Unborn Child by Orest Stocco
Perilous Panacea by Ronald Klueh
Last Song of the Whales by Four Arrows

If you are an author or prospective author who would like to be published contact Savant Books and Publications at

http://www.savantbooksandpublications.com